HIGH
PLACES

Julie Conrad

Published in 2021
by Julie Conrad

© Copyright Julie Conrad

ISBN: 978-1-913898-12-0

Also available as an ebook

Cover and Book interior Design by Russell Holden
www.pixeltweakspublications.com

Pixel Tweaks Publications
SELF PUBLISHING MADE SIMPLE

For my mother Rose Margaret Lyons-Whittle
and my husband and soulmate Alan
and our family of dogs past and present.

PROLOGUE

The sound of rattling keys. A nurse appeared at the doorway.

'Come along, Magda. You have a visitor.'

Confused and dazed, Magda slowly lifted her heavy body from the bed.

As they made their way along the grey, barren corridors, voices echoed, haunting cries of despair; the journey along those corridors seemed never-ending.

Eventually, she was led into a dull, cramped, austere office. Passing a small mirror on the office wall, she caught a glimpse of a woman's face. A face ravaged by grief and torment, a woman with no future, a woman she no longer recognised.

CHAPTER ONE

1990

Magda landed herself a prime position as a secretary at Simpsons Financial Services. It was her first real job in the City, straight from the Premier Secretarial College.

Her best friend, Emma Fairchild, had a secretarial position in the City too; she had started work for another prestigious finance company. Emma's father was a member of parliament and knew most CEOs in the City.

Would Emma have got the job on merit alone? Doubtful. The job hadn't been advertised.

Magda and Emma became friends from day one at the secretarial college. Magda was surprised to find most of the students lived in the inner zone of London, the affluent areas of South Kensington and Chelsea. She had managed to rent a small flat in the outer zone of London and was able to travel into the City by Tube. Aunt Lillian had loaned her money for accommodation and living expenses and had paid the college fees. Magda would have to wait until she turned twenty years old before she would have access to the trust fund left to her following the death of her parents; the money from the insurance company had been substantial.

Magda was a regular visitor to Emma Fairchild's family home in Putney. She envied Emma's stable family life; her father protected his family from the harsh realities of the outside world. The Fairchild's had embraced Magda as one of their own, as she and Emma were inseparable.

Magda had very few memories of her early childhood; she vaguely remembered her parents, just a hazy recollection.

She hadn't looked at the family photographs since their deaths. Aunt Lillian had put the photographs away. She thought it best; she didn't want Magda looking at them and pining for her parents. Instead, Magda was encouraged to put it all behind her and focus on her schooling and the future.

Not having parents to be proud of her, protect her and give unconditional love was hard. Aunt Lillian had provided well for her, but she could never fill the emotional void with the affection that Magda so deeply craved.

Magda thought Emma's father, Charles Fairchild, was an excellent example of the ideal man: he was tall, slim and eloquent, and always appeared in complete control and immaculately dressed. Yes, one day she would marry a man just like him. Maybe he would be a politician. He would adore her and she would never feel, or be, alone again.

1975

'Magda, darling, time for school.'

The Rainford family lived in Borehamwood, Hertfordshire. Mr Rainford worked away in the Middle East. Sometimes he was away for six months. Therefore, Magda and her mother spent a lot of time together.

'Magda, come along. You'll be late for school.'

While walking to school, Mrs Rainford thought it a good time to share some news.

'I received a letter from your father. He said the company have agreed to pay for my flight out to visit him. I don't want to take you out of school, so Aunt Lillian will come to stay with you while I'm away.'

'I don't want you to go.'

'It's only for three weeks, then I'll be back. Would you prefer to stay with Aunt Lillian in Wimbledon?'

'No. All my friends are here. When are you going?'

'In two weeks, time. It will fly by …'

'Oh, look, Mum, Jenny is at the school gates. Don't walk me all the way there.'

'Okay, but I will keep watch until I see you go through the gates.'

'Bye, Mum.' She ran to meet her friend.

'My family are attending a Conservative Party dinner coming up. There is a spare seat at our table –Magda would you like to join us?'

'Sounds interesting. When is it?'

'A week on Saturday. I know it's short notice but I immediately thought of you.'

'I bet it's a stuffy affair?'

'I don't think so – there's going to be a band and dancing.'

'Will there be other younger people?'

'Maybe, come along and find out.'

'Well, as I have a window in my diary …'

'Oh, you are funny, Magda. We'll have fun, we always do. Are you still coming round this evening?'

'Yes.'

'Great, we can talk about it then. I'll see you around six o'clock. Bring a change of clothes and stay over.'

Magda went straight to Emma's from work. In Emma's bedroom they put on music, Pet Shop Boys, and caught up on the gossip.

'Father told me the Prime Minister and all the cabinet members will be attending the dinner dance.'

'Really?' Magda tried to put a face to anyone in the Tory cabinet. 'What are you wearing?'

'An evening dress, I have a couple if you want to borrow one,' said Emma.

'A long dress?'

'Yes, don't you have one?'

'No, I've never needed one. Could I take a look at yours?'

Emma opened the wardrobe and pulled out the dresses. 'The emerald green is my favourite. It's the newer of the two.'

Magda picked up the blue dress and held it against herself. 'This isn't my colour at all. Thanks for the offer. I'll have to buy one.'

'Suit yourself.'

'So, everyone will be in an evening dress?'

'Of course, except the men.'

Mrs Fairchild came into the room with clean clothing that needed to be put away. 'What are you two giggling about?'

'Just one of Emma's lame jokes.'

'Magda is going to buy herself an evening dress for the dinner dance. I'll wear my green velvet dress unless Father decides he wants to treat me to a new dress especially for the occasion.'

'What type of dress should I look for, Mrs Fairchild?'

'Nothing fussy. Preferably in one colour – it will look more sophisticated. You don't need to spend a lot of money; you can add tasteful accessories to make it more stylish. Oh, nothing low cut, that wouldn't be appropriate.'

Patricia Fairchild breezed out of the room; her fragrance lingered in the air.

'Lovely perfume.'

'Chanel No. 5. Mum has always worn it.'

'Do you think she would mind if I wore the same perfume for the dinner party? It smells so sophisticated and grown up.'

'She won't mind. Anyway, the perfume will smell different on you.'

'Why?'

'All perfumes smell slightly different on each individual.'

Emma sat at her dressing table, brushing through her long, silky red hair. She was very pretty, with a pale porcelain complexion and large green eyes. Magda watched her, and thought how fortunate Emma was.

Emma had it all.

CHAPTER TWO

At eight o'clock, prompt, the Fairchild party arrived at the Grosvenor Hotel. A smartly dressed waiter offered Magda a glass of champagne. Among the introductions and small talk, Magda did recognise some of the faces. Past and present politicians. Some of the old guard, were unsteady on their feet. As the Fairchild's mingled, Emma and Magda went in search of more champagne.

'Gosh, this is good.'

'It's the good stuff all right.' Emma looked around.

'I wonder if there are any eligible young men here this evening?'

'I haven't seen anyone under fifty.'

At eight thirty an announcement was made.

'Ladies and gentlemen, please make your way to your table.' A table plan had been on display and the Fairchild's were to be seated on table fourteen. The large, round tables were elegantly laid and each person had been allocated a seat.

'Oh, look, Emma, our name places. I'm glad we are sat next to each other.'

Magda noticed that the top table was slightly raised. There was an excitement in the air. She had never been to anything so grand. The tension grew; a great deal of fuss was occurring at the entrance of the room.

'I think they are here,' Emma whispered.

'My lords, ladies and gentlemen. Please be upstanding for the Prime Minister Mr John Major and Mrs Norma Major.' Everyone was on their feet to give a standing ovation, which continued as the couple made their way to the top table. Magda didn't recognise anyone else at the top table but knew they must be important to be seated with the Prime Minister.

Waiters unobtrusively carried bottles of red and white wine, serving white wine first.

'Mr Fairchild, who are the people at the Prime Minister's table?'

'Well, Magda, to the left of the Prime Minister is the party chairman, Jeffrey Archer, and his wife, Mary – surely you have heard or seen Jeffrey before?'

'I'm not sure.'

'To the right is Sir John and Lady Winston, then Sir Rufus Holroyd, without Lady Holroyd. He is the member of parliament for Barnston Green, in Kent, and is guest speaker.'

Magda stopped listening. She was transfixed by Sir Rufus Holroyd.

Such a handsome man, she thought.

'A number of extremely wealthy businessmen are here. They donate large sums of money to the party.'

The Fairchilds' table included Sir Hugo Humphreys and his wife and two sons.

Sir Hugo was extremely overweight and his face so red it was almost purple. Magda didn't like Sir Hugo; he was loud and pompous. She avoided eye contact with him as he blustered on and on, hogging the conversation.

It wasn't the stuffy affair she had imagined. In fact, it was spectacular. She was dazzled by the many famous faces that started to appear, from the world of business and entertainment. All the men wore black tie and dinner jackets that made the most boring man look glamorous.

'Look, Emma, it's the chap who introduces *Top of the Pops*.'

'So it is. We'll go and talk to him later.'

After dinner, the party chairman rose to his feet. He thanked everyone for attending and continued with amusing conversation for a further fifteen minutes. Then it was time to introduce the guest speaker.

'My lords, ladies and gentlemen, I take great pleasure in welcoming, this evening, a man who has long served as a member of parliament for his local constituency of Barnston Green, Kent, a man who represents all that the Conservative Party stands for, a man of commitment and integrity. Ladies and gentlemen, I give you Sir Rufus Holroyd.'

Rufus rose to his feet as his audience applauded with zeal. Magda was captivated by this incredibly handsome man. She couldn't take her eyes off him, impressed by his eloquence and confidence. Most of what he was saying went straight over her head, but she was mesmerised by the man – six foot tall, lean yet muscular with a lightly tanned complexion, steel-grey hair and neatly trimmed moustache and beard.

His speech ended to much applause from an appreciative audience including Magda.

'I never imagined a politician could be so handsome.'

'Steady on, Magda, I'm a politician,' Mr Fairchild reminded her. The entire table roared with laughter.

Waiters offered more wine.

'I'm feeling a bit tipsy. I'll pass and wait for coffee and petits fours.'

'Good idea,' said Emma. 'I don't want you throwing up in my bedroom.'

The string quartet had played throughout the meal and as they quietly left the room the party chairman introduced the entertainer for the evening.

'Ladies and gentlemen, I would like to introduce a comedian who is no stranger to the Conservative Party dinner dances – he has entertained us many times. Back by popular demand, Mr Tim David.'

'He said he was a popular comedian. I've never seen him before.'

'You must have, he's been around for years.'

His gags were a bit blue but they got the laughs, and he really loosened up the audience.

The alcohol was having a wonderful effect on Magda; she could feel a warm excitement inside her. People were mingling and table-hopping.

'Let's go to the loo now before there's a queue.' Emma led Magda by the hand as they squeezed past people engrossed in conversation. Magda watched the ladies at the handwash facilities.

'Have you seen the jewellery these women are wearing? Diamonds the size of an egg.'

'And those lovely Dior bags. Before I forget – we're off to Provence over summer. Do you want to come with us?' Emma asked.

'What about work?'

'Ask to take three weeks' leave. We could leave the oldies and go off on our own for a few days, get the train to the coast.'

'Yes, I'd love to go to Nice and Saint-Tropez.'

'I'll tell Father you're coming.'

A drum roll echoed around the room, which got everyone's attention.

'Come on, something's happening out there.'

On stage, the band was tuning up.

'Ladies and gentlemen, I hope you are all having a great evening. We would like to introduce ourselves. We are Heston's Big Band. I am Heston and I am joined by Joe, Frank and Brodie on the drums. Say hello, guys.'

The band waved at the audience.

'We are here to entertain you this evening. I want to see you all on the dance floor. Is everybody ready to dance the night away?'

'Yes!' yelled the audience.

'Here we go.'

The Prime Minister and his wife were the first to take to the floor, quickly followed by the other guests.

People began to circulate and chat. Charles Fairchild gathered his family together.

'Before we hit the dance floor, I want to introduce you all to a few people.' As he ushered them towards the top table,

Magda couldn't believe her luck. Mr Fairchild was going to introduce them to Sir Rufus Holroyd.

Magda was the last to be introduced. She could feel herself blush her heart thudding so hard she could feel it against her chest. Rufus's eyes fixed on Magda while he spoke about things in general, allowing the Fairchild's to engage in the conversation, though his eyes would return to Magda.

Magda was sure Rufus was attracted to her. She could feel it. She had never felt this way before, ever. Noticing his blue eyes, how they danced and sparkled, both unnerved and excited her.

Throughout the evening she was aware of Rufus watching her; she pretended not to notice but couldn't resist looking his way.

In the powder room, she gazed at her reflection in the full-length mirror. She hardly recognised herself. The long, black fitted dress with a low back enhanced her slender figure. Her long hair was piled high on her head. She looked amazing and so grown up, a woman of the world.

On her way back to the table, people mingled and chatted making it difficult to pass by. A hand ran up and down her arm, making it tingle. She turned and found herself looking into those blue eyes. A smile beamed across her face.

'Hello again. It's Magda, isn't it?'

'Yes, you have a good memory.'

'Well, as you are the most attractive woman here it was impossible to forget.'

'Thank you.' The longer they stood face to face the more embarrassed she became. She was sure he could read her mind and knew what she had been fantasising about. Still smiling, he asked, 'What's your connection with Charles Fairchild?'

'I'm a friend of his daughter, Emma.'

There was a momentary pause, then in a jovial tone he asked, 'Are you interested in politics?'

'I don't know much about politics but I am willing to learn.'

'Maybe I could teach you.'

'Maybe?' Her breathing became rapid, her face flushed.

'Excuse me,' Sir Hugo interrupted. 'Rufus, I would like your opinion. My dear, would you excuse us.'

'Yes, of course,' she lied.

Rufus smiled; he maintained eye contact with her. Flustered, she returned to their table. She didn't get an opportunity to get close to Rufus again, but she was happy, very, very happy.

'Where have you been?' Emma asked.

'Having a chat with Sir Rufus. He is so lovely.'

'Well, forget him. Come on, let's dance.'

CHAPTER THREE

Rufus James Holroyd was the younger son of Sir Edward and Lady Margaret Holroyd. A child who came into the world when both parents were in their early forties. Sir Edward and Lady Holroyd were both from wealthy backgrounds and were society people. They frequently threw lavish dinner parties at their home, Grange Manor. The arrival of Rufus came as a shock to his parents. His mother found caring for a baby exhausted her, and so Nanny Barnes, who had nursed Edward junior, took responsibility. Although his early years were spent almost exclusively with Nanny Barnes, he never felt unloved or unwanted by his parents. He was a happy, emotionally stable child, who was allowed to attend garden parties and fetes, along with Nanny Barnes. The social whirl of his parents' lifestyle was perfectly normal to him. Rufus grew up as if an only child, as his brother, Edward junior, eleven years his senior, was at boarding school. Rufus always looked forward to his older brother returning home, for the summer break and for the festive season. By the time Rufus was sent to boarding school, his brother was making his way in the world of finance in the City.

1964

During the summer break, before going up to the University of Oxford to study law, Rufus spent time at home with his parents.

He awoke early, got out of bed and went over to the large French windows. He drew back the curtains and stepped out onto the balcony. It was a crisp, fresh, sunny morning in early September. Only a few more weeks before he left the family home.

Downstairs at breakfast, as always, the table was covered with a crisp, white table cloth. Lady Holroyd was taking her usual tea with lemon and wholemeal toast. Sir Edward took his tea with milk and always had scrambled eggs with toast.

Rufus had no set breakfast routine, but had set a new trend as the family's first coffee drinker.

'Good morning, Mother, Father.'

'Good morning, dear.'

'Eh, good morning.' His father returned to his newspaper.

There was little conversation at breakfast; his father read the newspaper and didn't like to be disturbed. However, this wasn't the case when Edward junior was staying over. He always had something of interest to talk about – he relaxed the atmosphere, often with laughter and banter. Edward was based in London and at twenty-nine years old was spending more time with his girlfriend. Rufus intended to follow in his brother's footsteps, he admired him so. Any mention of Edward junior and his parents' faces would light up.

A party had been arranged at Grange Manor, on account of Rufus being accepted by Oxford; it was a celebratory send-off for their younger son. Edward junior was bringing

Sophia, his girlfriend. The rest of the guests were long-standing family friends, some of whom were bringing along their daughters in hope of enticing young Rufus.

On the big day, Lady Holroyd was busy supervising the caterers. She had given Mrs Ronson, the housekeeper, the rest of the day off. Mrs Ronson had prepared the guest rooms before leaving.

'Rufus dear. Make sure you are here to welcome Edward, Sophia and her parents, Mr and Mrs Walker-Brown, at three o'clock.'

'Okay.'

Rufus hated fuss and formality; worst of all, the evening was for him. He went for a long run to get away from the hive of activity and burn up some nervous energy.

As he had expected, the dinner party was tiresome, just as they always were. The familiar bombardment of tedious questions and comments.

'Are you intending to have a career in law?'

'Back in the day …'

'Have you met a young lady yet?'

Lady Holroyd sparkled as usual; she came alive at social gatherings. His father monopolised the evening's conversation, speculating on Edward junior's bright future. Rufus didn't mind this in the slightest; it saved him from being centre of attention, which always made him feel awkward.

'Quiet, please. Ladies and gentlemen, I would like to make a toast on behalf of our younger son, Rufus, who will be leaving us shortly for Oxford. His mother and I are very proud of him and his achievements to date. We wish him every success and happiness in his future and if he does half as well as our other son, Edward, we shall be very proud indeed. Please raise your glasses, to Rufus.'

'To Rufus.'

Everyone stood silently waiting for Rufus to respond with a speech. He rose to his feet.

'I would like to thank my parents for arranging this wonderful dinner party on my behalf and to thank each and every one of you for attending, and for your good wishes.' He sat down. There would be no elaborate speech from Rufus.

'Edward, Sophia is delightful, you seem very happy together,' Rufus said.

'Thank you. She is very special.'

'I am so pleased for you.'

'You might meet your future wife at Oxford.'

'I'm in no rush to get married. Why is it that when a couple fall in love, they want everyone to be in love? They become matchmakers, setting up blind dates.'

Edward laughed. 'Because, dear brother, the euphoria of being in love is such a wonderful feeling, you just want to spread it around. I won't be trying to fix you up. All our female friends are way too old for you.'

'Good, I have a lot of living to do.'

Mrs Defoe shuffled between the boys. 'Rufus, you know my daughter, Clara.'

'Yes, I have seen Clara on a few occasions. Hello, Clara.'

'Hello, Rufus. Mother thinks it would be a good idea for us to be pen pals, so you have a girl back home.'

'I am going to university, not off to war.'

Mrs Defoe was undeterred. 'Clara is an ideal young lady for you. She writes so beautifully – do correspond with her. She will keep you updated on life in Barnston Green. Clara also has a beautiful voice, soprano.'

'I'm sure she has. Excuse me, I must circulate with the guests.'

Rufus swiftly joined his brother and Sophia.

'Edward, you abandoned me. I think Clara was going to burst into song. How cringy would that have been?'

'Move on, brother. They are making their way over here.'

* * *

The day before the start of term, Rufus travelled up to Oxford alone. His father had suggested his chauffeur drive him there, but Rufus didn't want to arrive feeling conspicuous, so he travelled by train with basic luggage. The rest of his belongings would be sent on during the week.

Rufus knew his life was about to change as he embarked on adulthood, but he still felt like a boy. He hoped he would make friends quickly; even as a boarder at school he had often felt lonely and at Grange Manor he had always had to make his own entertainment. Some friends from school would be at Oxford, but they would be at different colleges and would want to make new friends.

He quickly settled into his rooms and joined the other students as they all familiarised themselves with Brasenose College.

Rufus's room was across the way from two other boys. He decided to introduce himself.

'Hello, I am Rufus Holroyd. We are neighbours for the next year.'

'Hi, I'm Joshua.'

'Hello, I'm Robert. Good to meet you. We're just going for a walk – would you like to join me and Josh in the students' bar later?'

'I would love to.'

'Four o'clock, okay? We will knock for you we can go over together.'

There was also a number of attractive female students.

Rufus enjoyed having female company and was amazed by their intellect and forthright attitude. He hadn't met many girls before and certainly not such as these. Female companionship prior to Oxford had been the daughters of his parents' friends; they had been frivolous and superficial. He was reviewing his opinion of the opposite sex.

Rufus was making lots of friends, male and female, and together they all discovered alcohol, consuming great quantities of beer. On Friday evening they all got plastered. Rufus wasn't too keen on the taste of beer but he was fond of its effect. It also caused him to lose his inhibitions. He would wake up the following morning and get flashbacks of getting passionate with certain females. It was having to face them when sober that he dreaded. But these girls didn't seem to care, unlike the girls back home. It was no big deal they didn't expect an engagement ring.

'Excessive binge-drinking has to stop,' Rufus told Josh and Rob. 'I've joined a few of the university sports teams. I competed in the 800-metre run yesterday, I was out of breath and sluggish. Me, trailing behind, out of puff. That won't happen again.'

'Don't expect us to sign the pledge with you. I love a blast on a Friday,' Josh said.

'You enjoy a blast any day of the week,' Rob joked.

'I have always loved cricket, that could be my forte, I might be a professional cricketer or other sportsman,' said Rufus.

'We will come and cheer you on, Rufus, with a beer in hand.'

However, it was his interest in politics that became his passion.

Going along to the Young Conservative Society was the start.

'Hello, I am Rufus Holroyd.'

'Welcome, Rufus. Cedric Bowes-Water.' He held out his hand. 'In your first year?'

'Yes.' Rufus was very impressed by the chairman of the Young Conservative group.

'I am in my third and final year.' Cedric appeared and sounded much older than his years. He dressed formally and his hair was already beginning to thin.

'Have you made any career plans?' Rufus asked in awe.

'Politics, of course. I have a position at Conservative Party headquarters. I want to work my way up.'

'Do you want to be a member of parliament?'

'No, more civil service. That's the plan.'

'Best of luck, although I'm sure you won't need it with your knowledge and experience of politics. I have watched and listened to you in a few debates, you know your stuff.'

'We need more people to get active in the group. Are you interested in getting involved? It is a commitment, but if you love politics as I do, it will open doors in the future.'

'I would love to.'

'There is a committee meeting on Wednesday, 4 p.m., in tutorial room 16. Come along, meet the members. There will be a few positions on the committee coming up as three of us are leaving after sitting our finals.'

'I'll be there.'

The whole subject of politics fascinated Rufus – so much so, he became active within the society. Photocopying information and distributing it around campus, putting up posters, advertising forthcoming meetings and guest speakers. He enjoyed the debates, the arguments for and against economic and social policies.

His first term was flying by, his days full of lectures, coursework, politics, sport and women.

'Here he is with the beers. Clear the table.' Rufus put down the drinks.

'Fabulous, first of the day.'

'Gosh, Josh, its only four o'clock. You'll be asleep by eight o'clock.'

'Instead of hitting the bar every afternoon, why don't you both come along to one of our meetings?'

'Watch out, Rob, Rufus is on a recruitment drive.'

'I've no interest in Conservative Party politics. General politics, yes. But you won't get me dishing out leaflets and sitting in stuffy meetings.'

'Rob isn't even sure the law is for him yet, let alone politics.'

Rufus was surprised. 'How can you possibly not want to practise law or politics?'

'Very easily. I'm nineteen years old, I don't know what I want to be or do. Josh and I find it strange that you are so adamant that politics is the path for you. How can you know?'

'How can you not know? I just love it.'

* * *

Rufus returned to Grange Manor for Christmas; a familiar feeling of melancholy overwhelmed him. It would be the usual celebrations and routines. Christmas Day would begin with church, and they'd return home for the opening of gifts. Christmas dinner at four o'clock and the usual guests arriving at three o'clock, for aperitifs and nibbles. It was a very formal affair with all the old guard with whom his parents socialised. After a couple of glasses of sherry, the guests would start to repeat themselves, and ask him the same questions. It was like having an interview.

'Rufus, how are your studies going?'

'What career path are you considering?'

On and on, meaningless, pointless, tiresome questions. Rufus would be bored and lonely.

Fortunately, he had coursework to do and books to read.

Mrs Ronson met Rufus at the door.

'Good afternoon, sir. I saw your taxi coming down the drive. Lovely to see you again. Do you need a hand with your bags?'

'No, Mrs Ronson, I can manage. Nice to see you too.'

'Rufus, my boy, welcome home. Your mother is out with a friend – Harrods, last-minute Christmas shopping. Come in, get warm by the fire. Mrs Ronson, would you fix Rufus a hot drink and a sandwich, please?'

'Of course. Coffee; cheese and onion sandwich?'

'That would be great, thank you, Mrs Ronson.'

'Good news, Rufus. Edward is joining us Christmas Day and says he has a surprise for us.'

'Father, that's great.'

'I can't wait to tell your mother he is joining us. She will be delighted.'

Rufus was cheered by the news. Edward would lift the mood; he had the ability to loosen up his parents, who were otherwise so stiff. Edward loved the limelight, which took the heat off Rufus.

Edward, and Sophia, arrived early on Christmas morning.

'Mother, Father, stay indoors. It's freezing out here.'

'No, let me help you with your luggage.' Sir Edward helped his son bring in the bags.

'Come through and get warm by the fire, dear.' Lady Holroyd was pretty sure she knew what the surprise was going to be.

Mrs Ronson took their coats, while everyone sat down to catch up.

'Shall I serve coffee, Lady Holroyd?'

She nodded her approval. 'We are looking forward to your surprise, Edward. Are you going to put us out of our misery?'

Edward smiled at Sophia. Then he stood up.

'Mother and Father, as you know, Sophia and I have been together for some time now.'

'Well, spit it out man,' Sir Edward joked.

'Sophia is now my fiancée.'

'Oh, congratulations, darling.' Hugs and kisses and joyful chatter followed.

'May we look at the ring?'

'I was trying to keep it covered with my hand until Edward had made the announcement.' Sophia thrust her hand forwards.

'Oh, my dear, it is beautiful.'

'We chose it together, didn't we, darling?'

'Yes, Sophia wanted a solitaire. I was happy with whatever she wanted. This ring was the most spectacular.'

'It's certainly that.' Sir Edward smiled. 'We must mark the occasion.'

Sir Edward disappeared and returned with a bottle of champagne.

'Just a small one to toast the happy couple. Then off to church.'

He was followed by Mrs Ronson, with champagne glasses.

'Mrs Ronson, would you give Rufus a call please, tell him to join us.'

'Yes, Lady Holroyd.'

While the family celebrated with their son and future daughter-in-law, Rufus made his way downstairs.

'Hi, Edward, so glad you're here.'

'Rufus, meet your future sister-in-law.'

'My goodness, this is a surprise. Father said you had something special to share, but this is the best news ever. Welcome to the family, Sophia. My brother is the best.'

'Thank you, Rufus, you are all very kind. Yes, I know he is one in a million.'

Lady Holroyd smiled; her heart swelled with joy and pride.

'I am so glad Edward has met such a beautiful young woman. We knew this day would come.'

'Rufus, your champagne.'

'Raise your glass to Edward and Sophia.'

'Edward and Sophia.'

The good news was shared with the vicar, Mr Townley, who shared it with the congregation. Whether it was because of the good news or the champagne, Sir Edward almost lifted the roof singing the hymns with gusto. It made all the family smile. It was turning out to be a very sociable, happy Christmas after all.

* * *

Happy to be back at Oxford with his friends, Rufus was re-energised. Spring term was going to be productive both academically and politically.

'Look, guys, I will go wherever you decide. I just want to get as far away from home as possible.'

'Well, I vote Thailand.' Robert put up his hand.

'Why not,' Josh agreed. 'We can't keep putting off a decision.'

'Me too.' Rufus cheered.

'Summer days are calling us, guys.'

Monday morning's lecture was taken by Mr Day. He taught the history of law, and he made the subject fascinating. Josh and Robert sneaked in late and sat at the back. Rufus smiled to himself – so typical of the boys to be late on a Monday morning.

A student entered the room, interrupting the lecture, spoke with Mr Day and then left.

'Silence, please. Rufus, the Dean must see you in his office.'

'Right now?' Rufus asked.

'Yes, straight away.'

Josh and Robert looked over at Rufus, who shrugged as he passed them.

What does the Dean want with me? I haven't done anything wrong. Feeling a mixture of foreboding and fear, he left the room.

Rufus knocked on the door and was asked to enter.

The Dean, Professor Stanhope, looked very sombre.

'Please take a seat, Rufus.'

'I have some very bad news. I have just received a telephone call from your father. There has been an accident, a car accident in Spain.'

Rufus, confused, stared at the professor as he continued.

'Your brother, Edward, was in that accident. I am afraid he was killed.'

Rufus sat in silence, trying to take in what had been said.

'I have no other information at this point. You, of course, will need to go home. Your father is sending his car for you; it should arrive at four o'clock. I suggest you go back to your room and pack a few things.'

Rufus rose to his feet. 'Edward is dead?'

'I am afraid so. I am truly sorry for your loss.' Professor Stanhope bowed his head.

Rufus went to his room and lay on the bed. He went over and over what Stanhope had said. It didn't seem real. He remained motionless on his bed all afternoon until his father's chauffeur arrived.

Markland paid his respects. 'I am sorry for your loss, young Rufus. Edward was a fine young man.' He helped Rufus take his luggage to the car. 'Anything I can do to help the family you only have to ask.'

'Thank you, Markland.'

Once he was seated in the back of the car, the reality of what had happened began to sink in. Rufus could feel the emotion rising; he muffled his tears as long as he could, before he gave way to sobs. Markland remained silent throughout the journey home.

Why did this have to happen to Edward? It just wasn't fair.

They approached Grange Manor; the grey skies matched the sombre mood. As he entered the house, he could feel the grief in the atmosphere. He looked around. There was only silence and an emptiness.

Sir Edward greeted his son with a big hug.

'Rufus, your mother has taken the news very badly. She is beside herself with grief. Dr Parks visited earlier and administered a sedative, so she is resting in her room.'

Rufus had never seen his father upset before – he had never seen him show any emotion – and he was quite shocked by his father's appearance. His face and eyes were red and puffy from crying; he must have been crying for hours to look the way he did.

Sir Edward's voice was broken as he said, 'I am going upstairs to join your mother. When the sedative wears off, she will need me by her side.' Hurrying to the stairway, he turned. 'Rufus, the staff won't be in until tomorrow. You will have to fix yourself something to eat.' Then he was gone.

Bewildered, Rufus went to his room. It was gloomy and depressing. The weather was grey and cloudy while inside the Grange it was cold, dull and mournful. He didn't know what he had expected on returning home but he had never thought it would be like this, the end of the world. Again, he was alone, alone in his room.

What was he supposed to do? He found no comfort at Grange Manor, nor from his parents, his poor grief-stricken parents, whose grief was so intense it scared him.

Edward junior had been the light of their life and now that light had gone.

Early the next morning, Rufus went downstairs; he could hear activity in the kitchen.

'Mrs Ronson. Any chance of a cup of coffee?'

'Oh, my dear boy, of course. I am so sorry for your loss. Your brother, Edward, was such a good, clever boy, never any trouble to your dear parents.'

He couldn't wait to get away from her.

'Yes. Thank you. I will be in the breakfast room.'

A few minutes later Mrs Ronson appeared with coffee and a plate of toast.

'I'll leave you in peace.'

Relieved to be left alone, he took his coffee cup and a slice of toast and went outside. It was bliss to be out of the house, in the fresh air. It was early spring and the birds were singing, the tulips were coming into bloom. Everywhere was bursting into life, a new cycle of life was emerging. Little birds would be flying the nest for the first time very soon, a butterfly fluttered around the garden, young squirrels chased each other from tree to tree. He sat at the little table to have his breakfast. The world outside was in such contrast to the world he and his family inhabited at this time. It didn't seem right that such beauty and new beginnings could be happening when death and grief was blanketing the family.

He walked around the grounds and into the meadow, taking deep breaths. He found it hard to breathe, he gulped in the air, but the more he tried to fill his lungs the harder it became. He fell to his knees and broke down and cried.

Sir Edward wandered from room to room, aimlessly, trying to find something, anything to distract him from the pain. He went into the kitchen to give instructions to the staff on what needed to be done.

'Mrs Ronson. Lady Holroyd will be taking breakfast in her room until further notice. Would you prepare her something?'

'Of course, Sir Edward. Will she be wanting her usual?'

'Yes, thank you. I will take it to her. She doesn't want to see anyone.'

'I understand, sir.'

Sir Edward and his wife withdrew into themselves, sharing their grief with no one but each other.

Up with the lark, the next day, Rufus cycled into the village. Nothing had changed, same people with the same routines. Although lonely, he didn't want to engage in conversation. It seemed too much effort, all that pointless chat. He pushed his bicycle along the pavement. Elderly people were mingling around the post office doorway, the same near the local supermarket. People with sad expressions on their faces nodded towards him. Rufus nodded back.

Major Rook's daughter approached him.

'Oh, Rufus, I am so sorry to hear about Edward. You must all be devastated. Do give my condolences to your parents.'

'Thank you. I will.' Not wanting to discuss the matter further, he tried to move on.

'It must be absolutely awful for you. I have never lost anyone close ... well, an old aunt who I couldn't even remember. I suppose your parents are dressing in black, the colour of mourning, like Queen Victoria when she lost Albert …'

He was starting to feel breathless. His chest tightened.

'I really must get on my way.'

'We are here if you need anything,' she called after him.

Rufus got back on his bike and cycled through the village and on to the country roads. He cycled as fast as his legs were able to peddle; he sped along the lanes, the wind blowing through his hair. He wanted the wind to blow away all the negativity that clogged his head, all the depressing thoughts that consumed his brain.

Returning home, in the late afternoon, his legs heavy from cycling and his whole body weary from exertion, he put his bike away and went indoors. Sir Edward was sitting passively in the hallway.

'Are you okay, Father?'

'No, I must say, I have never felt so bad in all my life.'

'Sorry. It was a stupid question.'

'Rufus, Mrs Ronson has laid out your suit, it is in your room. Edward will be brought to the house at nine fifty-five, before leaving at ten o'clock.'

'I'll be ready, Father. How is Mother?'

'Inconsolable.'

Rufus did not see his mother until the morning of the funeral. Her only acknowledgement of him was a quick glance, while Sir Edward continued to fuss around her protectively.

Rufus had stepped forwards to embrace her, but she gently waved him away. She stood like a statue, frozen, still. She wore a large hat and dark glasses; she wanted to remain remote from everyone, especially the mourners waiting at the church. She had no wish to engage in conversation with anyone.

Rufus was troubled by the look in her eyes. Was he over-reacting, or did her eyes betray her thoughts? Did they say, why could it not have been you? Rufus felt such sorrow. He pushed the thought out of his mind.

The funeral service was carried out by the vicar, Mr Townley. It was heart-breaking to see so many of Edward junior's friends from school, university and work, in attendance with their wives and fiancées. Edward junior's fiancée stood in the front pew with Sir Edward and Lady Holroyd. Some of the local people gathered at the back of the church.

Mr Townley opened the service.

'Dearly beloved, we are gathered here today to say farewell to our dearly departed Edward William Holroyd. I have known Edward all his life. As an infant he was christened at this church and I saw him grow into the successful, generous man he became. Edward was a regular fundraiser for our parish church, usually by seeking sponsorship for his numerous marathons and triathlons.

'I was looking forward to conducting the ceremony at his forthcoming marriage to his wonderful fiancée, Sophia, next spring. Alas, it is not to be.

'We do not always understand the ways of the Lord. He has taken our dear Edward at a time when so many joyous possibilities lay before him, and although we grieve the loss of our brother, we must trust in the Lord above, that his death is not in vain.

'If you turn to your hymn book, we will begin with a hymn very special to Edward's mother and father. We shall sing "Jerusalem".'

The small choir helped along the reluctant congregation in singing the hymns. It would have been a poor version of 'Jerusalem' without them.

Sir Edward walked to the front of the congregation to read the eulogy.

'Edward was our first born, and we thought the last until Rufus came along eleven years later, a surprise or a miracle baby, I think they refer to it as being.

'Edward, from being a toddler, was inquisitive, sweet natured and brought us great joy. At school he excelled academically and was a great sportsman. Never short of something to say, he would tell the funniest stories when he returned home from boarding school and university. He was still filling our lives with joy, up until the phone call informing us of his passing. It fills us with great sadness that he will never get to marry his loving fiancée, Sophia. Never have the children they had planned to bring into the world. Never reach his full potential as a human being.

'Edward, my son, our son, will be a great loss to everyone who knew him and those who had yet to meet him.' Sir Edward began to splutter.

'His mother and I shall miss our boy until the day we die.'

Looking at the congregation, he said, 'We love you, Edward, our special boy.'

Tears streamed down his face as he re-joined his wife. He held her hand tightly.

A close friend of Edward's was next to come forwards to say a few words. He relayed stories of their escapades while at school, which brought a little lightness and a few smiles to the ceremony.

Mr Townley continued to direct the service.

'Our final hymn, "Abide with Me", will be followed by the Lord's Prayer.'

The final hymn left a sombre atmosphere within the church. The family were not ready to celebrate Edward's life. They still wanted him back.

Bringing the service to a close, Mr Townley had the last word.

'May the Lord bless you and keep you. May the Lord's countenance shine upon you, this day and forever more. Amen.'

Mr Townley shook hands with everyone as they left the church. He tried to give a few words of comfort to the Holroyd's.

'I am here seven days a week if you need to talk or pray. I will visit you both at home, you only have to ask. The community grieves with you today.'

'Thank you, Mr Townley.'

Sir Edward ushered his wife to the car. Markland held the door for her and she quickly disappeared behind the tinted windows of the vehicle.

Sir Edward looked around for Rufus.

A reception had been arranged at a local hotel. Lady Holroyd did not want anyone at Grange Manor. She didn't want to hear platitudes or any more condolences. She was going home, alone.

'Rufus, you will have to attend the wake by yourself. I must take your mother home. I thought she might change her mind and attend for a short time, but she feels unwell.'

'Of course, Father. What about Sophia?'

'She and her parents are going straight home.'

'I will head over shortly.'

'We appreciate you doing this on our behalf.'

The hotel was full of people and many kind words were spoken in Edward's memory, though no words could comfort the family. As family representative, Rufus went through the motions of thanking people for travelling from far and wide to attend the funeral. He was not only grieving for his brother, but also for himself, having realised that Edward was much more than his parents' favourite son. He was their life. They hadn't loved them equally. He had lost his brother and his parents in the wake of Edward's death.

The next hour he spent on autopilot. As he watched people drinking more and more wine, they became louder and more animated. Laughter, jokes, catching up with old friends and acquaintances – the wake had taken on a party atmosphere.

Rufus knew they didn't mean any disrespect. Life goes on. He was glad his mother wasn't there.

He slipped away.

Rufus packed his bags and carried them downstairs ready for the morning. Sir Edward walked into the hallway.

'Everything go okay?'

'Yes. I stayed an hour and then left them all to it.'

'I see your bags are packed.'

'Father, I'm heading back to university tomorrow.'

'That's for the best, get back to your studies. Thank you, for taking charge this afternoon. Your mother and I appreciate it. There is little else you can do here. I assume you're leaving early?'

'Yes, eight o'clock train.'

'Have a safe journey back to Oxford.'

'Thank you.'

Rufus matured overnight. He began to question everything, nothing was as he thought it was, even life itself.

'Sorry we didn't get to see you before you left. We were shocked to hear your brother had died,' Rob said.

'It's okay, boys. The funeral is over, Edward has gone.'

'We are very sorry for your loss, Rufus,' Josh stressed.

'I know you are. Thank you. I need to get back to some sort of normality.'

'Come on, let's go for a drink.' Both boys draped an arm over Rufus's shoulder and led him to the bar.

Rufus started to take greater interest in life and events outside his own insular world. For the first time, he became aware that there were millions of people throughout the country and the world not as fortunate as him, people who did not perceive life as he did. He had come to the conclusion that if one's life could be snuffed out so unexpectedly, then one should use one's time on this earth as productively as possible. This was the point at which the seed of altruism was planted inside him.

Although he would always love his parents, things between them would never be the same. He saw them through new eyes. He became critical of their judgemental, frivolous lifestyle and of their friends and political bias.

His thoughts turned to Nanny Barnes. When he was sent to boarding school, Nanny Barnes had been kept on in order to supervise him over the holidays. He reflected on how important she had been in his life; she had always been there for him. Rufus had taken her for granted, that she had been put on this earth for the sole purpose of raising him. What sort of life had she had? No husband, no children of her own – had she felt abandoned when her services had no longer been required? Nanny had played a significant role in his life, providing love, care and security.

He wasn't like his parents, nor was he like his brother, Edward.

He was his own man.

CHAPTER FOUR

Rufus was now sole heir to Grange Manor, which did give him some satisfaction, but for now he would put his family and home behind him and focus on his studies. Many of his fellow students, particularly in the Conservative society, were surprised that not only was Rufus intelligent and astute, but that he also possessed a social conscience.

Cedric Bowes-Water, having graduated from Oxford, had remained in touch with Rufus. They had become extremely good friends. Cedric married his university sweetheart, Penny, and was making a name for himself in the political world. He now worked in a government department that liaised with the intelligence agencies.

Cedric invited Rufus to join him and his wife at a charity ball, an extravagant affair.

'Rufus, so pleased to see you.'

'Cedric, a little bird tells me your work involves a close liaison with the security services.'

'Who's been talking?'

'I couldn't possibly say.'

'I think I can guess the culprit – was the little bird my dear wife, by any chance?'

'Darling Cedric, you take it all so seriously,' Penny said.

'I do hope you haven't told anyone else.'

'Rufus isn't just anybody.'

'I say, Rufus, it's a sad state of affairs when you can't trust your wife to keep shtum.'

'I promise not to tell anyone else.'

'My dear Penny, I don't intend to share anything confidential with you. You see, Rufus, she finds it all so amusing.'

Penny kissed her husband on the cheek and then went to join a couple who had just arrived.

'Rufus, there is someone I would like you to meet. Follow me.'

Following Cedric, Rufus thought it might be a political heavy weight, as Cedric was now mixing with the great and the good.

'Rufus, may I introduce you to a dear friend of mine? This is Lindy Rostron, and like you she is studying at Oxford, reading English literature.'

'Delighted to meet you, Lindy.'

'Likewise. Cedric should have told me sooner he had such a handsome friend.'

Lindy wore mid-heeled shoes that added to her tall, statuesque physique. She was pale-skinned and wore her blonde mane of hair swept up high on her head. Rufus and Lindy hit it off immediately and talked to the exclusion of others for the next ten minutes.

'What are you thinking, Rufus?' she said, fixing him with her beautiful blue eyes.

'That you are a very confident woman.'

'Do you like confident women?'

'I certainly like you.'

'What are you going to do about it?'

'You will have to wait and see.'

'As much as I enjoy being in your company, handsome man, I must speak to some of my dear friends. Come and find me in a while.' She kissed him lightly on the cheek and sashayed away.

Re-joining the party, Rufus was smitten.

'Cedric, she is amazing.'

'I see Lindy has knocked you off your feet. She is pretty amazing.'

'She is dazzling, bewitching.'

'Ah, the poet within you is emerging. Yes, she is all those things. She is also headstrong, opinionated and always right.'

'I could live with that.' Rufus was hooked.

'Don't say I didn't warn you.'

From that evening onwards they became a couple. Rufus was so proud of Lindy. She could hold court with any group of people. She was challenging and assertive.

He admired her strength and independence. She was forthright and spoke her mind. He had never met a woman like her. He thought about her all the time; she brought a smile to his face. He wrote poems from the heart, to express the way he felt.

Both Rufus and Lindy were busy with their studies and involved in different groups and societies. They made an effort to meet up whenever possible and always at week-ends. Being on different campuses didn't help. Lindy was up with the lark; she preferred to wake up in her own bed, so rarely stayed over with Rufus. She also needed eight hours' sleep. Rufus, on the other hand, was a night owl and never went to bed before the early hours. He cycled over some afternoons on the off-chance of her being around. If she was busy or at a lecture, he would post a poem under her door.

Today, she was there.

'Are you busy?' Rufus asked, as he propped himself against the door.

'I am trying to get this assignment finished for tomorrow. You may come and sit quietly, if you wish.'

'I just wanted to drop this off for you.'

Her expression spoke volumes.

'Oh, Rufus, you haven't written more poetry? Look, they are stacked up – these are still unread and now you have brought another one.'

'I didn't realise it was such hardship, to read a poem.'

'I have important things to read.'

'You are reading English literature, I thought you would enjoy them.'

'Dear Rufus, I do enjoy reading the works of the great poets, but your poetry is, to put it gently, rather soppy. I don't think the syllabus will ever include the poetry of Rufus Holroyd, do you?'

'My poetry is especially for you. It isn't soppy, it's romantic, it's how I feel about you. Every word is true.'

'That's all very well, but I'd rather you didn't write any more. I know you mean well and your heart is in the right place, but this is not the time. What if someone else should read them? They will think I am in a relationship with a big softy.'

'I can see you're busy. I'll leave you to it.'

'Catch you later, darling.' Lindy didn't bother to look up as he left.

With a bruised ego and his confidence waning, he decided to stop writing about his feelings in poems and prose. Lindy clearly thought them ridiculous. Perhaps they were.

As the months went by, Lindy became more demanding and he found he was expected to explain himself to her and had to justify doing anything that she disagreed with. He was miserable most of the time and he dared not look in the direction of another woman should Lindy make more out of it.

What had first attracted him to Lindy? It struck him that shortly after meeting her he had felt as though he had known her a long time and he had found this comforting. Recently, however, he had noticed a shallowness and selfishness to her personality. She was wearing him down. Then, like a bolt from the blue, it suddenly hit him why she seemed so familiar to him: she was a carbon copy of his mother.

Lindy and Rufus took a walk around the park.

'Rufus, you're miles away, come back to me.'

'I was thinking.'

'Well, don't. What must you not forget?'

'I can't remember.'

'Rufus, are you deliberately trying to annoy me? About Friday.'

'Enlighten me.'

'You have, you've forgotten about my little soirée on Friday evening. I have invited a group of friends I want you to meet. Drinks, nibbles, interesting conversation and debate.'

'I'll be there.'

However, Rufus had made the decision to stop seeing Lindy. Their relationship wasn't working out, being in her company brought him no pleasure anymore. He had promised to be there, so he would go, but this would be the last time they would spend together as a couple. He would broach the subject when a suitable opportunity arose.

Dreading the evening ahead, he turned up deliberately ten minutes late. Lindy believed in punctuality, so he knew she would be displeased, but after he got through the evening, he would be free of her.

The party was in full swing when he arrived. People were smoking; the room was full of smog. He started coughing and waving it out of his face.

'Rufus darling, where have you been, you're late?'

Without giving him the opportunity to answer she grabbed his arm and began to introduce him to her guests. One by one he made a little small talk as their names drifted over his head until …

'Rufus dear, this is Daphne. She is staying with me for two nights, I told you all about her.'

Lindy's voice seemed to disappear into the ether as he gazed at the beautiful woman stood before him. He was bewitched.

Conversation with Daphne was so easy; he warmed to her sweet nature and gentleness. Time passed in the blink of an eye.

'Come along, both of you. Time to join the group discussion. Come along, Rufus.' Lindy took his hand and led him away, while calling out, 'I'm sure Daphne can pretend to understand what we are discussing. Just nod and smile, dear.'

Rufus whispered into Lindy's ear. 'That's rather cruel of you. I thought she was your friend?'

'Do you ever listen to a word I say, Rufus? Daphne doesn't mind, she knows me too well. She is my sister.'

'She's your sister?'

'Yes, I have told you about her a number of times. See, you never listen.'

It was like a blow to the stomach. He looked over at Daphne, who smiled at him. The news had put a spanner in the works but it wasn't insurmountable. He had to see this girl again, he just had to.

Throughout the rest of the evening, he kept looking towards Daphne and they would smile at each other. He felt as if Lindy had him on a lead – he was expected to follow her around and be available to join in the various discussions with her guests.

The party was coming to a close. He went over to Lindy's desk, tore a small piece of paper from a pad, and jotted down a message. While everyone was saying their farewells, he took Daphne's hand in his and pressed the folded piece of paper into her palm. It read, *'I hope you won't think too badly of me, Daphne, but I would love to see you again.'*

Lindy came up behind him, wrapping her arms around his waist.

'Time you were leaving, my love. I am glad you have met my sister at last. After all, we may all be related in a few years.' She kissed Rufus on the cheek.

'Goodbye, Rufus. It was lovely to meet you.' Daphne smiled.

He hoped she didn't think he was some kind of a cad or a seducer of women. He had to see her again. Hopefully, she would agree to see him and then he could explain.

Rufus agonised throughout the week, as he played out in his mind different scenarios of what might happen, until the letter he had been waiting for arrived.

There was hope. Daphne had suggested she meet him at Oxford train station on Saturday at twelve noon.

Rufus's mood swung from elation to despair as he continued to imagine different outcomes. What if she rejected him? She could have done so in the letter, but what if she wanted to give him a piece of her mind? But why would she come up to Oxford to do so? Or she could be making the journey to drop in on Lindy and to tell her how ghastly he was. As he counted down the days, the wait was unbearable.

With a spring in his step, Rufus arrived early at the train station. Pacing up and down, he could hardly contain his excitement and fear. The twelve-noon train pulled into the station, and as soon as their eyes met, he knew everything would be okay. Smiling, Daphne took his arm, and they strolled quietly out of the station. They walked and talked, as they made their way towards the centre of Oxford, oblivious to the world around them until finding themselves outside the Randolph Hotel.

'Let me reserve a table for afternoon tea. In the mean-time we can wait in the bar and have a drink or two.'

Two hours and a couple of white wines later they took their seats in the dining area and were served afternoon tea. It was time to address the elephant in the room.

'I know this is awkward. I truly like you, Daphne, and I had no idea you were Lindy's sister when I passed you the note. It was only later she told me you were sisters. I intended to end things with Lindy before I met you. We're not compatible. She is too … forceful for me. We haven't been getting along.'

'You don't need to explain. I know what Lindy is like.'

'As long as you understand.' He took her hand.

'So, what do you suggest we do?'

'If you and I are going to be seeing each other, I will need to explain the situation to Lindy as soon as possible.'

'You haven't told her yet?'

'I haven't seen her all week. We can go days without seeing each other.'

Daphne looked down into her lap.

'I've disappointed you,' he said.

'I assumed you would have dealt with the matter before I arrived.'

'I should have.'

'You weren't waiting to see what my reaction was, before ending it with Lindy?'

'No. I was going to end it with Lindy whatever your decision was.'

'So, what's the plan?'

'I will tell Lindy as soon as I can, tomorrow.'

'Will we be seeing each other exclusively, as a couple?'

'Yes, of course, that's what I want. Is that what you want too?'

'Yes, I do.'

They smiled and he leaned over and kissed her on the lips for the first time.

'More tea, sir, madam?' the waitress asked.

'Yes please.'

Time flies by when having fun. Daphne looked at her watch.

'Rufus, I need to be on the five o'clock train home.'

'Couldn't you stay over until tomorrow?'

'I think it best I go home. You have a lot to sort out with Lindy, and my parents would want to know if I was staying over with Lindy, and if not, where was I staying. It would get too complicated and I don't want to lie.'

'Promise me you won't change your mind about us?'

'No, never.' She squeezed his hand.

On Sunday morning, still loved up from the day before, he felt an urgency to end his relationship with Lindy.

He cycled over to her campus. It was eleven o'clock; she would be up and about.

'Rufus, what a lovely surprise. Sorry I haven't seen you but I have been busy studying for my exams. You do understand.'

'Yes, of course I do. Lindy, I need to talk to you.'

'Sounds serious. Before you say your piece, I need to say, I hope you weren't offended by what I said about your poems. It was ungracious of me. I was busy focusing on research, for my course.'

'It is a lot more serious than that.'

'Oh, my goodness, I think I know what you're going to say.'

'I don't think you do.'

'I hope you're not going to get down on one knee. I know you are so old-fashioned and romantic. You're not, are you?'

'Lindy, please.'

She started to laugh. 'Oh, you are?'

'Please, let me speak.'

'Wait. I take back what I just said. If you really want to get down on one knee, I won't hold it against you.'

Like a rabbit in the headlights, he froze.

'Rufus, are you all right?'

'I am just going to come out with it.'

'Oh, Rufus, say it, ask me.'

'I didn't come here to ask you anything, but to tell you something.'

The enthusiasm drained from Lindy's face. 'Tell me what?'

'This relationship, our relationship, isn't working.'

'Of-course it is, what are you talking about?'

'It isn't, Lindy, not for me.'

'What's your problem?'

'I don't have a problem.'

'You must have a problem, because I thought everything was hunky-dory. Why haven't you said anything before?'

'It wasn't the right time.'

'Rufus, sit down. Tell me what's bothering you and we can work it out.'

'There is nothing to be done, our relationship is going nowhere.'

'Well, at least tell me what the problem is?'

'It's you, Lindy, my problem is you.'

Rufus was taken aback by how bitterly she reacted. He had never for a minute imagined Lindy had fallen in love with him.

He cycled back to his campus feeling bad. He hadn't wanted to hurt her.

After pulling up abruptly, he parked up his bike and went to Robert's place.

'Rob, do you have five minutes?'

'Sure, come in.' Robert was busily scribbling notes.

'Just a minute of your time.'

'Sorry, Rufus. Just had to get this information down or I'll forget it.'

Rufus, shuffled, he was twitchy and needed to off load.

'I've ended it with Lindy.'

'Oh, I'm sorry to hear that. I thought you two were for keeps.'

'Don't be sorry, I'm not.'

Rob, sensed his friend was unsure of himself.

'What's the problem?'

'Why does everyone keep asking me that? I don't have a problem. Things aren't right between me and Lindy. I realised she isn't the one for me.'

'Calm down, it makes no odds to me. It's your decision.'

'I didn't mean to jump down your throat. Sorry.'

'It's okay.'

'I have met someone else, someone kind, considerate and wonderful.'

'That was quick.'

'These things just happen when you least expect them to.'

'All right, it's not a criticism.'

'Sorry, again.'

'You have met someone new – that's good, isn't it?'

Rufus looked down at the floor. 'She's Lindy's sister.'

'Oh, my goodness. That's not good.'

'I have to see her. Daphne, Daphne, is her name.'

'What did Lindy say?'

'She threw me out when I told her it was over.'

'No, I mean when you told her about her sister.'

Rufus remained quiet.

'You haven't told her?'

'No.'

'If you are serious about dating her sister, you have to go back there now and tell Lindy everything.'

Rufus did just that. The worst was over; she knew they were finished. He just had to get over the next hurdle.

'Lindy, please let me in, I need to talk to you.'

Lindy opened the door.

'Come in. But if you want forgiveness, I'm afraid I won't find it easy to—'

'There is something else I must tell you.'

'You haven't come back for forgiveness, have you?'

'No.'

'Surprise me – oh, let me guess, you have met someone else?'

'I have.'

Lindy's face crumpled.

'I have to tell you who it is.'

'Why? To rub salt in the wound? Why should I care who she is?'

'It's Daphne.'

It took a few seconds before the penny dropped.

'As in my sister Daphne?'

'Yes.'

'But you only met her a week ago. How can this have happened?'

'The moment you introduced me to her, we just clicked. It's not an ideal situation, but I'm sure we—'

'Not ideal. It is an impossible situation. How could this have happened? Did you both discuss this at the party?'

'No. I took the lead. When the party ended and I was saying goodbye to her, I passed her a note, asking if I could see her again.'

'Daphne stayed with me for two nights and never said a thing. And did she say she would see you again?'

'Yes, in fact, we met up Saturday afternoon.'

'What? Why didn't she tell me?'

'Don't blame her.'

'Where did you meet?'

'She came up by train.'

Lindy was livid. 'My boyfriend was meeting my sister behind my back on Saturday.'

'It wasn't like that.'

'Did it not cross your mind that dearest Daphne only wants you because you're mine? She has always been jealous of me. I am the clever one, the sociable one, the beautiful one. You would leave me for her?'

'I had decided to stop seeing you before I met her. I just hadn't told you.'

'So, I am the last to know.'

'Don't blame her, I asked her out.'

'What she has done to me is unforgivable.'

'But she is your sister.'

'Not anymore, she is no sister of mine. You have both been conspiring behind my back. I will never accept you and her being together. I will never forgive either of you.'

She got to her feet and walked towards him. She slapped him hard across the face.

'I hate you and I hate her. I will never accept what you both have done to me. Never.'

Rufus saw his chance to get away. He thought it was all rather extreme and that time would be a great healer. Anyway, he was too much in love to lose any sleep over a woman scorned.

Rufus wrote to Daphne immediately to tell her that he had told Lindy everything and that she wasn't too pleased. He also wrote Daphne a romantic poem, which he sent with the letter.

Daphne wrote back, relieved it was out in the open. She accepted the poem graciously. From that day forth he wrote to Daphne twice a week, giving an account of his day. It wasn't like it had been with Lindy; he had resented giving her an account of his comings and goings, but he enjoyed telling Daphne. He wanted to share every moment with her.

Rufus was deeply in love and Daphne was all he could think about.

Lindy was distraught. She went to the only person she felt able to tell.

'Lindy, what are you doing here? Whatever's the matter?'

'Cedric, I need to talk to you.'

'Come in and sit down. You look as if you need a brandy.'

'No, a tea will do. I am not going down that slippery road because of him.'

'Because of who?'

'Rufus. He has ended our relationship.'

'Why? What has happened?'

'He's met someone else.'

'I am so sorry, Lindy. I am as shocked as you are.'

'He hasn't said anything to you?'

'No, nothing.'

'Did he say who she was?'

'Daphne.'

It took a few seconds for it to register. 'Daphne? Your Daphne?'

'Yes. Neither of them said anything to me. It started at my little party on Friday evening, a week ago. I will never forgive them.'

'Friday evening. That was quick work, impetuous, but that's Rufus, the romantic. It could all go pear-shaped.'

'Even if it did, he isn't going to come back to me. You should have seen his face. He didn't care about my feelings.'

'You're an attractive, intelligent woman. You will meet someone else.'

'No, I won't. I love him. I will never feel the same for anyone.'

Cedric took her in his arms as the tears flowed. 'My darling girl, let it all out.'

'I can't bear to be alone, I only trust you with my deepest feelings, I don't feel able to tell any of my other friends. I feel such a fool.'

'No one will see it that way.'

'I do. So, they will. I introduced them, for goodness' sake. I can't even go to my mothers' home as that bitch is there.'

'Then, you must stay here. Penny won't mind; she is very fond of you.'

'I'll be no bother. I just can't bear to be on my own.'

'Stay as long as you like. We're out at work during the day.'

'Just a couple of days. I have exams very soon and I have no intention of fucking them up because of those two wretches.'

'That's the spirit.'

Cedric was disappointed in Rufus. Bad enough ending the relationship with Lindy so brutally, but to announce he was seeing her sister in the same breath was not gentlemanly at all.

He had introduced them and Rufus had treated his dear friend so shabbily, so unlike him, or he had thought.

He would help Lindy pick up the pieces.

CHAPTER FIVE

Rufus was in his final year at Oxford and Christmas was looming; he decided it was high time he introduced Daphne to his parents. The Holroyd's agreed that Daphne would join the family for the entire Christmas week at Grange Manor. Daphne was excited about meeting Rufus's parents. Her own parents had divorced three years ago – now they would not need to argue over which one of them she stayed with over the festive period.

Daphne's stay at the Grange was a pleasurable one. The Holroyd's had guests for dinner, on both Christmas Eve and Christmas Day. Lady Holroyd took time to speak with Daphne and made her welcome. She spoke at length about Edward junior.

'We are still in touch with Edward's fiancée, Sophia. We went to Sophia's wedding, would you believe. We were very sad when she told us she was getting married, but knew she couldn't put her life on hold forever. She and Edward were the perfect couple. They could have had a wonderful life together.'

'I am so sorry, Lady Holroyd.'

'Come, I'll get out the photographs of the boys when they were young.'

Both women pored over photographs of times gone by.

'I am so pleased Rufus has found himself such a charming companion. I am sure we will have time to talk again during your stay. If you would excuse me, I have to attend to our other guests.'

'Yes, of course.'

The Christmas week at Grange Manor allowed Rufus and Daphne to spend a lot of time alone together. They went riding and walking, and they made love for the first time while his parents were out visiting. Although the earth didn't move, it was an intimate bonding experience. As they lay in each other's arms, Rufus suggested that they get engaged. Daphne needed no persuading.

New Year's Eve was celebrated with a few close friends of his parents'. It was the first time Rufus and Daphne would be letting in the new year together. Rufus tapped on his glass to get everyone's attention.

'Mother, Father and all our guests here this evening. I have an announcement to make.'

Everyone looked surprised.

'I have asked Daphne to marry me and she said yes.'

There was silence. Then a burst of activity.

'Congratulations, both of you. Daphne, we would be delighted for you to be part of our family.' Sir Edward reached out and shook hands with Rufus and hugged and kissed Daphne, quickly followed by good wishes, hand-shakes and embraces from the guests.

Sir Edward was in a cheerful mood from a mixture of wine, sherry and a brandy.

'This evening we are welcoming in a new year and celebrating Rufus and Daphne's engagement.'

Striking midnight, the grandfather clock began to chime. Fireworks filled the sky, vibrant colour and sparkle stretched across the night.

'Daphne, you have made me the happiest man alive.'

A year after Rufus's graduation, at the age of twenty-two, he married Daphne. The ceremony took place at the local parish church.

Lady Holroyd had arranged the flowers beautifully and had talked at length to Mr Townley about how the ceremony should be conducted.

Daphne's mother and sister sent their apologies as they would not be attending the wedding. They had been invited to go skiing at Aspen by Lindy's new beau, an eligible bachelor named James Forsyth Brown, as in the wealthy Forsyth Brown family. It was believed that he would propose to Lindy on this vacation. An investment not to be missed, thought a shrewd Mrs Rostron.

Mr Rostron, Daphne's father, and his new lady friend would represent the family at the wedding. The only thing the divorced Mr and Mrs Rostron agreed on was that it was imperative both girls be married as soon as possible. Security was what both girls needed.

Mr Rostron made it to the church on time to give his daughter away, cutting it rather fine. His female companion was a much younger, attractive woman, who joined the families on the front pews. Daphne was secretly relieved her mother and sister had been unable to attend as they would have created an atmosphere; at least she and Rufus could relax and enjoy their day. She had known that Lindy would never have attended.

Every bride should look radiant on their wedding day and Daphne was no exception. Her wedding dress was made of ivory satin, silk and lace flatteringly fitted at the bodice. She had chosen to have only one bridesmaid, her dear childhood friend Juliet, whose dress was also made of satin in pale lilac. Both Daphne and Juliet had bouquets of white roses and violets.

Rufus had chosen Cedric Bowes-Water to be his best man; they both dressed in grey morning suits and top hats. Rufus was tall with a lean, muscular body while Cedric was smaller and slight of frame. Cedric was five foot and eight inches tall but looked smaller at the side of Rufus. Cedric's thinning hair had all but disappeared, but one could still tell he was a young man.

Sir Edward looked nothing like his son Rufus; he was much shorter and quite portly. Edward junior had been very much like their father in build and appearance. Rufus resembled his mother's side of the family. Lady Holroyd looked a picture of elegance; she was still so slender, her fair hair whisked up into a chignon. She was wearing a pale blue suit that brought out the blue in her eyes and complemented the porcelain translucence of her complexion.

The church was filled with so many family friends. Rufus had been so pleased to see his parents had prepared and arranged his wedding day with such enthusiasm. What really made his day was seeing Nanny Barnes seated with the family in the front pews. Her face filled with joy and pride on seeing Rufus arrive. He leaned over and kissed her.

'Nanny, I am so pleased you are here today. It makes it twice as special.'

'You deserve every happiness, my dear boy.'

Excitement buzzed through the congregation as the organist began to play the wedding march. Mr Rostron proudly escorted his daughter down the aisle.

Mr Townley welcomed the congregation.

'We are here today to witness the joining in marriage of Rufus James Holroyd and Daphne Rostron.'

Rufus and Daphne said their vows, their eyes filled with emotion. They knew this was love that would endure whatever was thrown at them.

Outside the church the photographer got everyone together and explained what order the photographs would be taken in, starting with bride and groom alone and then with best man and bridesmaid, before moving on to family and friends.

'Where is the mother of the groom?' he called.

Sir Edward had a good idea where she was.

'Leave it with me, I'll find her. Powdering her nose, no doubt.'

He walked to the rear of the church.

'Margaret.'

'I just had to come and see him, to tell him we miss him.' She rested her hand on the headstone.

'We will always miss him, but today is for Rufus, it is his big day. Let's go and do him proud.'

'Edward should be here.'

'I know, but he isn't. Let's go and join everyone.'

'Of course.'

'Come along, Margaret, we need you in the photographs.'

They hurried back.

'I have found her.'

Everyone cheered.

Rufus spotted two dear friends with their plus ones.

'Josh, Robert, over here. Mother, Father, I would like to introduce you to my good friends from Oxford, Joshua and Robert.'

'No one ever refers to me as Joshua.'

'Official introductions – my mother's a lady, don't forget.'

Josh did a mock curtsy.

Sir Edward instantly liked the boys.

'Welcome, it is a pleasure to meet you at last.'

'It's so nice to put faces to names.' Lady Holroyd smiled.

Josh called over the girls. 'Rufus, this is Adele, my better half.'

'How do you put up with him?' Rufus joked.

'He is an acquired taste.'

'This is my fiancée, Ruth.'

'Rob, you're engaged? When's the big day?'

'Maybe next year, we've not decided. I see Daphne was the real deal after all.'

'I never doubted it, Rob.'

'Is the sister of the bride here?'

'No, best not to mention anything.' Rufus was taken aback by the mention of Lindy; she was in his past.

'You will all meet Daphne at the reception. See you later, boys.'

The reception at Grange Manor was a spectacular affair. A string quartet played throughout the lavish meal and everyone appeared in good spirits and full of joy and happiness for the newlyweds.

Cedric remarked to his wife, 'Did you see the outlandish hats those women were wearing? They would be more appropriate at Royal Ascot.'

'Cedric darling, you are such a traditionalist.'

'Are you trying to say I am old-fashioned?'

Cedric's wife was lively and jovial company. She had hit it off with Rufus on their first meeting; she was so pleased he had found his soulmate.

The speeches were varied. Mr Royston excelled himself and did Daphne proud, his confidence in abundance knowing his ex-wife was thousands of miles away. He was thoroughly enjoying himself. He ended his speech by saying, 'I could not ask for a better son-in-law than Rufus. I know he will love and care for Daphne and she for him. They will make each other very happy for the rest of their lives together. What more could any man want for his daughter?'

Cedric's speech was witty and affectionate. He described Rufus as 'The sort of chap everyone would want as a friend. A man of compassion and integrity. He will make a wonderful husband and one day he will be a brilliant politician.' Penny nudged her husband. He always had to bring politics into every situation, even a wedding.

Rufus was already the prospective party candidate for his local constituency.

Cedric finished his best-man duties by reading out messages from those unable to make the big day, including a message from Aspen.

Rufus got to his feet.

'I would like to start by thanking each and every one of you for being here today, to share our joy and happiness. I want to thank my parents – in particular my mother, who has arranged absolutely everything on our behalf. She has been amazing.

'I want to thank my now father-in-law for his wonderful speech and for his permission to marry his beautiful

60

daughter. Also, my best man, Cedric Bowes-Water, the best friend I could ever ask for. To our bridesmaid, Juliet, for carrying out her duties to perfection. Last but not least, I wish to thank my now wife, Daphne, who has made today the happiest day of my life.'

Everyone applauded.

Sir Edward said, 'Please raise your glasses, to the bride and groom.'

Everyone rose to their feet.

'The bride and groom.'

The newlyweds honeymooned on the Greek island of Crete. On their first evening they sat on the sand and gazed at the stars. Daphne turned to Rufus.

'You don't wish that you were here with Lindy, do you?'

He looked at her in disbelief. 'I cannot believe you said that. What on earth made you ask such a question?'

'I'm sorry, I know it sounds stupid, but ...'

Rufus took her hand. 'I love you and only you, forever.'

She squeezed his hand; she understood.

CHAPTER SIX

1990

It had been two weeks since the dinner dance and out of the blue a letter arrived addressed to Miss Magda Rainford. It was no ordinary letter; she noticed immediately the quality of the envelope and recognised the Houses of Parliament emblem. Excitedly she tore it open, knowing it was something special. She wasn't disappointed. It was from Rufus Holroyd: an invitation.

Magda was thrilled. She wanted to tell the world but intuition told her she should keep this to herself. She wouldn't even tell Emma ... well, not yet.

Rufus had invited her to the Houses of Parliament, neutral ground. He would give her the grand tour. Magda saw any chance of romance disappearing. *It's not a date – just an invite and I'm a guest.* Deciding to make the most of the experience, she accepted the invitation.

Arriving on time, she was about to ask an official for help when she saw Rufus walking towards her.

'Magda, welcome.'

'Thank you for inviting me.'

Rufus was the perfect host as they toured the Houses of Parliament. He gave a potted history and introduced her to a number of people. After meeting and greeting, smiling and nodding to all and sundry, she was pleased to be invited to his official office. His secretary arranged tea and biscuits.

Rufus poured the tea. 'Biscuit?'

'Oh, yes please. All that walking has given me a need of a sugar boost.'

'It was a lot to take in.' He smiled.

'Yes, I enjoyed it. I cannot thank you enough for taking time out of your busy schedule to escort me around this amazing place.'

She thought how marvellous he was. Charming, engaging and full of energy and enthusiasm.

'Do you love your work?' she asked.

'Yes, I can say without hesitation that I love what I do. I never doubted I would have a career in politics. How about you? Do you enjoy your work?'

'Yes, very much.'

The conversation was grinding to a halt.

'I should let you get on with your day. I will be on my way.' Magda got to her feet.

'I can't let you go so soon, after travelling in to meet me. Please, join me for dinner. We could get an early table.'

'Oh, yes that would be great.' Magda was delighted.

'I have a few things to attend to. If you could give me an hour or two, I should be finished by six o'clock.'

'No problem. I will go for a walk and get some fresh air. I will meet you at the main entrance. Two hours?'

'Excellent.'

Magda was thankful it wasn't raining. Taking a stroll across the bridge, she couldn't help but keep smiling to herself.

At six thirty they arrived at a little Italian restaurant in Covent Garden and sat at a table by the window.

'Tell me about yourself, Magda. You already know quite a bit about me.'

They shared a bottle of wine and Magda was feeling chilled.

'I'm an only child. My father worked as an engineer in the Middle East. He was away most of the time, so it was mainly me and Mum. When I was five years old, Aunt Lillian came to look after me, as Mum was going out to join Dad for a few weeks. To cut to the chase, my parents were killed in a car accident and so they never came home. I mean, I know they couldn't come home but ...'

'I understand.' He placed his hand over hers.

'I thought it was my fault. I know it wasn't but I still have this uneasy feeling of guilt.'

'It wasn't your fault. It was an accident.' He squeezed her hand.

'It was so sudden. The company arranged for their ashes to be returned home. They were interred in the local ceme- tery. Aunt Lillian took me to see the small gravestones but I couldn't associate them with my parents.'

'I am so sorry. That is a lot for a young child to experi- ence.'

'It was a long time ago. Aunt Lillian became my legal guardian and I lived with her in Wimbledon until moving further into London just over two years ago. I'm sorry for rambling on – I haven't spoken about it before.'

'No, please don't apologise. It was brave of you to open up to me. I feel privileged that you felt secure enough with me to share this part of your life. It's important to talk about these things.'

'I suppose it is.'

Rufus poured them both another glass of wine. 'I would like to make a toast to us both. May our futures be blessed with good fortune and happiness.'

He paid the bill and they walked side by side out of the restaurant.

'Would it be okay with you if we exchanged telephone numbers?'

Magda was surprised but pleased.

'Yes, why not, I'll jot down my home number and work number.'

'Could I borrow your pen?' Rufus wrote down a number. 'Well, it has been wonderful getting to know you. Shall I call you in the week?'

'That would be great.'

He kissed her lightly on the cheek and they went their separate ways.

Magda was sure her life would be full of promise from this moment on.

CHAPTER SEVEN

Rufus rang Magda almost daily, and a friendship grew between them. They would meet for a stolen hour in the Covent Garden area, to walk, or for lunch or a snack after work. The General Store café in Covent Garden became a regular meeting place. Their meetings always began with a peck on the cheek.

'Hi, Magda. Good day?'

'Yes. How about you?'

'Yes, especially now.'

Magda wasn't sure how to take some of his comments. Perhaps they were just innocent remarks.

'I took the initiative and bought you a coffee.'

'Thank you, Magda. I have been thinking a lot about you. Tell me more about yourself.'

'What do you want to know?'

'Pick up where we left off. When did you leave your aunt's?'

'I left Aunt Lillian's at the age of eighteen and went straight from school to the Premier Secretarial College, where I met Emma. Aunt Lillian had done her research and said the college had an excellent reputation. She paid the tuition fees and my accommodation and living allowance. I did pay her back. I had to wait until I turned twenty years old before I was able to access my trust fund. It was the insurance payment following the death of my parents.'

'What about Aunt Lillian, is she still in your life?'

'Aunt Lillian's health has deteriorated; she has Alzheimer's disease. I was in the middle of my course when she started to go downhill. I did visit occasionally. She had become forgetful, but then she deteriorated quickly and became a danger to herself, leaving her front door open and allowing strangers into her home who then stole from her. She started to wander outside in the middle of the night in her nightwear.'

'Was there no one to care for her?'

'Aunt Lillian was widowed in the Second World War and never married again, and therefore she had no children.'

'So, what happened next?'

'Social services got involved and assessed her needs. They told me she needed twenty-four-hour supervision and I agreed that she should be placed in a residential care home.'

'That must have been upsetting.'

'Yes. Aunt Lillian's solicitor dealt with the sale of her house and the funds from the sale pays for the homes fees.'

'Do you visit her?'

'I did visit a few times. I was shocked by her rapid decline. She became incoherent and couldn't remember who I was. She remembered Magda the little girl but had no idea I was the same girl.'

'So, you stopped going?'

'Yes. Does that make me a bad person?'

'No, of course not.'

'I found it depressed me. Every time I visited it brought back memories of my childhood – the intense feelings of loss and fear. I used to get short of breath and start to panic. I just couldn't keep going back there.'

'I understand.'

'Aunt Lillian always said that I should look to the future and not look back. So, I did.'

'I admire your strength and willpower to overcome the past.

'I do understand, Magda. Although my parents have passed away, I didn't feel any closeness towards them following the death of my older brother, Edward. When he passed away it became clear that he was their golden boy. I think I always knew it but it didn't matter when he was alive because I loved him too. After his death I had nothing in common with my parents, the common denominator had gone, Edward was gone.'

'It must have been difficult.'

'The experience changed us all. Things never remain the same between people, we constantly change and evolve.'

'I have so enjoyed talking to you, we are like birds of a feather.'

He covered her hand with his. 'You are a tonic, Magda, refreshing.'

'Thank you.'

'When shall I see you next?'

'We could meet for lunch next week?'

'I would like to take you out for dinner.'

'That would be lovely.'

Magda visited the Fairchilds' home less often, usually when Rufus was unavailable. She had acquired a certain amount of sophistication and an understanding of the social strata.

Magda wondered why Rufus had never mentioned his wife during their heart-to-heart conversations, of which there had been many.

Arriving at the Fairchild's home later than planned, she was bubbling inside with excitement as she joined Mrs Fairchild in the sitting room while waiting for Emma.

'We haven't seen you for a while.'

'I've been busy at work and doing overtime.'

'Emma has missed you. You are always welcome to stay over and go to work from here.'

'That's so kind. I get so tired. I get home, have a bite to eat, watch TV and go to bed.'

'Emma told me you enjoyed the dinner dance.'

'Oh yes.' Her face grew warmer. 'The guest speaker was very interesting. I was wondering why his wife wasn't with him.'

Mrs Fairchild looked up from the magazine she was flicking through. 'Daphne Holroyd doesn't come up to London very often.'

So, her name is Daphne. If only he was a widower or divorced.

'But he was guest speaker, I'm surprised she didn't make the effort to support him. Unless they go their own way?'

'I shouldn't think so. Apparently, they have a beautiful home set in acres of land. Hardly surprising she doesn't want to leave the place. Men in prominent positions such as Sir Rufus are invited to so many events and functions, it would be impossible for her to attend them all.'

'Do they have children?'

'No. It's just the two of them. I believe they are devoted to each other.'

That's what you think, Magda thought.

CHAPTER EIGHT

At eight o'clock, as arranged, a chauffeur-driven car arrived. Magda had chosen her dress carefully. She had kept it simple but classic: a black dress, just above the knee, with black tights and shoes, and a simple string of pearls, which gave her a more mature look. Her shoulder-length hair was glossy and youthful, her make-up minimal while focusing on her eyes – kohl and mascara enhanced them, making them appear large and shiny. While being driven to her destination, she was very nervous, and she remained silent throughout the journey. It was no longer a fantasy or day dream; she was about to be in the company of a fascinating man. She knew that wherever this was to lead, there would be consequences. Still, it was only an invite to dinner, wasn't it?

The car pulled up outside a central London apartment building. The chauffeur opened the car door for her to alight, his face expressionless. She approached the entrance of the building. Rufus stepped forwards to meet her. He greeted her like a long-lost friend. Although extremely excited, she felt immediately at ease in his company. The way he looked at her made her feel beautiful and desirable.

'I thought I would invite you in for an aperitif.' He sent the car away.

Magda followed him into the apartment. It was quite small, full of boxes and files.

'I work here most of the time.' He took her coat and she sat down. Rufus poured champagne into two crystal flutes.

'Thank you.'

'I thought we might dine here this evening. I ordered in for us. I do hope you like my choice.'

'I'm sure I will.' Magda was so excited food was the last thing on her mind.

Quite early on in the evening, Rufus laid his cards on the table.

'I assume you already know that I am married. I have been married to Daphne for over twenty years. I am at my apartment during the week and usually return to Grange Manor, the family home, at weekends, work permitting. I say the family home as that is where I grew up. My parents left Grange Manor to me and my wife.'

He paused.

'I think you know my feelings and intentions towards you and I would understand if you chose to walk away right now, should you be uncomfortable with what I have proposed.'

'Rufus, let's just enjoy the evening and see where it leads us.'

Magda awoke from a blissful sleep. Rufus was the first thing to come into her mind. It was like a dream come true. She was on cloud nine and in love for the first time. She went straight to the shower. As the hot water spray caressed her body, all her senses had been heightened. She was becoming aware of the sensuousness of her body. She only had to think of Rufus and intense waves of desire filled her being. She had never known such feelings; it was a sexual awakening. After putting on a robe and wrapping a towel around her head, she sat on the sofa with her first coffee of the day, her tummy doing somersaults. She couldn't eat a thing.

The door-bell for her flat rang. *Who on earth is calling so early?*

She went down to the communal entrance and opened the door. There stood a small man with a big grin on his face.

'Good morning, madam. Miss Magda Rainford?'

'Yes.'

The man disappeared to his van and returned with an extremely large bouquet of flowers.

'Wait one minute, miss.' He returned with a second bouquet of twenty-four red roses.

'Have a nice day.' The little man winked at her and went on his way.

'Wow. I certainly will.' Carrying the two bouquets back to her apartment, she took the small envelope from among the red roses and tore it open. The message read, *'Thank you for a wonderful evening R. x'.*

There was a second envelope in the bouquet of flowers. It read, *'Saturday 8pm? Love R x'.*

Overwhelmed to the point of bursting, she danced around the room. He had sent her two bouquets and wanted to see her again on a Saturday evening when he usually returned home. He had signed the message 'love'.

If she had had any doubts about why a sophisticated, cultured, prominent man like Rufus wanted to spend time with her, she didn't now. 'Maybe he loves me.'

She dressed quickly and left for work feeling truly alive and truly in love. How she had underestimated the power of love.

'Good afternoon, Simpsons Financial Services, may I help you?'

'Magda, it's Emma. How are you?'

'Good, thanks.'

'There is a fundraiser on Saturday for the Young Conservatives—'

'Sorry to interrupt, Emma, but I'm busy Saturday evening.'

'But we might meet Mr Right. Do you get it? It's a joke – Mr Right, as in right wing. Magda, are you still there?'

'Yes, I'm still here, but the answer is still no.'

'What could you be possibly doing that's more entertaining than an evening out with your best friend and lots of young guys?'

'I've made other arrangements.'

'Really? Anyone I know?'

'No.'

'So, it's a guy?'

'I can't go into it now and I'm at work. I need to go.'

'We don't have secrets, do we? But if you would rather keep it to yourself …'

'It's not a secret, I'm just unable to say anything about it, but you will be the first person I tell.'

'Sure.'

'I'm sorry to let you down, but it's something I can't cancel. I really enjoyed the dinner dance at the Grosvenor.'

'That was weeks ago. It will be at least another year before the next one.'

'The guest speaker, Rufus Holroyd wasn't it? He was a good speaker.' Magda tried to sound casual.

'Was he?'

'Yes, he was. What do you know about him?'

'Not much. Why?'

'Just interested that's all.'

'I know he is extremely well off. Do you fancy him?'

'Gosh no, don't be silly.'

'Good, because he is too old and he is married.'

'No, nothing like that,' she lied. 'I have to go. I will call you next week. Bye for now.'

Magda was relieved to end the conversation. She had already said too much.

No one must spoil this. She had never met anyone like Rufus before – handsome, sexy, eloquent, so sure of himself. Although they were from very different backgrounds, they shared a sense of belonging to each other.

Why let something such as him being married interfere with her happiness?

It was Saturday evening, seven thirty, and Magda was a flurry of excitement. She so wanted to present herself as a cool woman of the world. Instead, she was chasing her tail, behaving like a school girl, hot, flustered and in a total panic. She knocked back a large gin and tonic before stepping into her newly purchased, figure-hugging, burgundy dress. The new dress was a little more daring, more provocative than usual, a little low cut. She felt a bit ill at ease in her new seductive attire and it crossed her mind to change into something else. Unfortunately, at seven forty, the doorbell rang. The chauffeur was early? She dashed down the stairs to tell the chauffeur to wait a few minutes, which would allow her to change into the old faithful black dress. Opening the door, for a split second she was speechless. There was no chauffeur; instead, on her humble doorstep stood Rufus. Tall, handsome and sexy, with such a presence she felt as though she was going to faint.

Everything about Rufus spelt quality. He smiled. His straight, white teeth were enhanced by a light tan; his well-trimmed moustache and close-cut beard showed signs of greyness; his vivid blue eyes penetrated deep into her very being.

'Good evening.' Rufus looked bemused.

'Er. Hi.'

'I'll just get my coat.'

Rufus followed her into the hallway. 'You look stunning.'

She ran upstairs into the apartment, grabbed her coat, and re-joined him in the hallway. He walked towards her and pulled her into his arms and began to kiss her. Then he led her by the hand to his car, a dark grey Aston Martin V8.

It was cosy and warm. Beethoven played quietly on the car radio. Magda looked through the window into the cold, dark evening. It mirrored where she felt she had been most of her life, but not tonight. She felt warm and safe, excited and special. While driving he made small talk and she found herself reaching out for his hand. Very seriously she said, 'I really do like you. Well, more than like you. I want you to know that.'

Rufus gripped her hand and squeezed it. 'The feeling is mutual.'

'The fact you are married doesn't change the way I feel.'

He turned towards her briefly, smiled, and kissed her hand. Snuggled into her seat, relieved that she had expressed her feelings, she hoped that at some point he might announce that his marriage was on the rocks. She glanced through the window into the darkness and then looked back at Rufus and smiled to herself. Apart from the gold band on his finger, he was perfect.

Rufus drove into a car park.

'Darling, we are here.'

'Darling' he had said. It made her feel so special. As they walked towards the entrance of the restaurant, he slipped his arm around her waist, sending a tingling sensation up and down her spine.

'Good evening, Sir Rufus. Your table is ready. Please follow me, sir, madam.'

They were led to a table that was perfectly situated for an intimate evening, giving them an excellent view of the entire restaurant. The décor was superb; the tables were dimly lit with a single candle creating a very soothing atmosphere.

Rufus was captivated by Magda's youthful exuberance. She possessed an innocence untouched by worldly desires, such as greed or for material gain. Nor did she express any of those awful attitudes or behaviours such as jealousy, bitterness, resentment and hate, those emotions that rob a woman of her virtue and beauty.

He enjoyed showing Magda affection. He ran his finger along the side of her face and under her chin, tilted it, kissed her lips.

'You are so beautiful.' He rested his hand on her knee, and then moved it up, stroking her inner thigh. Her eyes widened. Magda flushed and pushed his hand back down to her knee. He removed his hand and poured them both another glass of wine.

'This is a very upmarket restaurant.'

'Don't you like it?'

'I love it. Do you come here regularly?'

'Yes, I used to, usually for the odd meeting. Although, I haven't been for quite some time. It is nice to be back, especially with you.'

They left the restaurant at eleven thirty and made the journey home.

'You are very beautiful.'

'Thank you.'

'You're very sexy.'

'Am I?'

The country roads were deserted and he slowed down the car, pulling off the road into a leafy lay-by. He switched off the engine and they undid their seat belts. They lowered the backs of their seats and lay back listening to the classical station. The wine had relaxed them; it was as if only they existed in the entire world. He sat up and leaned against the car door.

'Take off your shoes.'

She removed her shoes. Rufus pulled her legs towards him, resting them across his knees. Magda pressed her back against the car door; her body began to give in to the passion as he slowly ran his hands up and down her legs. Massaging her shins, her knees, his hands moved up and pressed hard against her thighs. She closed her eyes and, breathing deeper and slower, opening her eyes, she gasped. Magda was partially in shock but largely in ecstasy, even though she was twenty years old she had never been this far before and had certainly never been all the way. Did all couples do this so early in a relationship? Rufus seemed to have expected it. The sensation was indescribable. Panting for breath, eyes closed, she knew for sure that was the ultimate – this was an orgasm. The 'Big O' that all the magazines talked about.

After a pause, he said, 'We had better get you home.'

She smiled.

They travelled home in silence. Magda considered herself to be a woman now, and she knew that very soon, they would go all the way.

She no longer worried that she was out of her depth with Rufus, that she might come across as immature or stupid. When she was with him, she could be herself. He liked her to be herself; he preferred the simplistic, uncomplicated way she was.

CHAPTER NINE

Magda and Rufus had been spending a lot of time together, all be it for short periods at a time, but a closeness was developing and they had become familiar with each other's ways, likes and dislikes.

'Simpsons Financial Services, how may I help you?'

'Magda, a call for you. It's a Sir Rufus Holroyd.'

Her heart missed a beat. 'Hello.'

'Are you free this evening?'

'Yes.'

'I will pick you up at eight o'clock.'

'Where are we going?'

'It's a surprise. That's all I'm willing to say. Oh, and you can dress casually. I hope you like it and I hope you say yes to the surprise. See you at 8 p.m. Must go, darling.'

Magda beamed from ear to ear. *He hopes I say yes. Could it be a marriage proposal for after he divorces Daphne?* She couldn't think of anything else.

The telephone rang again. She grabbed the phone as if her life depended on it, thinking it was Rufus.

'Is this Simpsons Financial Services?' the fraught voice enquired.

'Yes, sir, how may I help you?'

Back to reality.

Back at her flat in Earl's Court, the telephone rang.

'Are you coming over this evening or shall I come to you? I haven't seen you in ages.'

'Not this evening, Emma.'

'Why? Even Mother and Father are wondering why you haven't been round. You're not ill or anything?'

'No, I'm fine. This evening I'm out meeting a friend.'

'May I join you?'

'No. Sorry.'

'You haven't got a new best friend?'

'You're my best friend.'

'You must be going on a date. Who is he?'

'It's not what you think.'

'I don't know what to think. Why are you being so secretive?'

Aware that time was ticking on, Magda said, 'I have to go. I will ring you later.'

'Later? What time?'

'Look, I don't know.'

Emma hung up.

At almost eight o'clock, she took a last look in the mirror. Black ski trousers tucked into black ankle boots, a white shirt blouse and a little waistcoat enhancing her tiny waist.

The door-bell rang. She ran her fingers through her hair, giving it a loose, sexy look, and hurried to the door with jacket, bag and keys.

Rufus looked sexier than ever. He looked at her adoringly.

'Hello, gorgeous. Ready?'

As they drove along, Magda filled with anticipation. 'Give me a clue?'

'No.'

'Are we going to a theatre?'

'There is no point in trying to guess where we are going.'

'I never realised that surprises could be so annoying.'

'Not much longer to wait.'

'Are we going to the Chelsea restaurant again?'

He said nothing. He turned in to a private car park behind an apartment building and parked the car.

'Come on.' He took her hand and led her into the plush building. They took the lift to the second floor.

'What are we doing here?' They carried on along the corridor and stopped outside apartment ten. He took out a key from his pocket and opened the door.

'Follow me.'

Had he borrowed the apartment for a night of passion?

'Have a look around and tell me what you think.'

'It's a wonderful apartment.'

'Keep looking around.'

Bewildered, she walked through the spacious lounge. The apartment was carpeted throughout with a deep-pile, cream-coloured carpet. The furniture was expensive. A beautiful mahogany dinner table with elegant tall-backed chairs. Magnificent long draped curtains screamed quality.

The bedroom was white-walled with watercolour paintings in the style of Monet. A white dressing table with a luxurious mirror and mirrored wardrobes. Last but not least the bathroom – it was sensational. A grey marbled bathroom suite, which included a jacuzzi, with roman pillars strategically placed to add style and panache.

Rufus was in the kitchen, the smallest room in the apartment but twice the size of her own kitchen. He was looking rather pleased with himself.

'This place is sensational. I have never seen anything like it. Who does it belong to and why are we here?'

'I want your opinion on the place.'

'Why?'

'I value your opinion.'

'Are you thinking of buying it?'

'No.'

'Who lives here?'

'A lovely lady.'

'Well, she's a very lucky lady.' Why bring her to a 'lovely' lady's apartment? 'Who is this woman?' she asked, feeling flat and annoyed.

'You know her.'

'I don't know anyone who lives in Chelsea or anyone who would live in such an exclusive apartment.'

'Yes, you do. Go into the hallway and look at the name on the keys.'

Sighing, she trotted off to get the keys. She was certain she didn't know this damn woman.

She picked up the keys and looked at the tag. Her heart began to thud. She hurried back to Rufus.

'I don't understand. It has my name on the keys.'

'Yes.'

'But …'

'This is the surprise. This is your apartment. If you want it.'

She gasped.

'If I want it?' She paused. 'I want it.'

Back at Magda's small flat, he told her he was unable to stay for long.

'Time for a coffee?'

'Yes,' he replied, looking at his watch. 'I don't want to leave the car outside for long. It stands out too much around here.'

They sat on the sofa. He kissed her gently.

'Why did you get me the apartment?'

'Because you deserve somewhere better than this place. It's also less conspicuous for me and my car to visit you in Chelsea.'

'Does that mean we are a couple and that you intend us to be together for some time?'

'I certainly do, if that's okay with you?'

'Yes.' She hoped it was going to last forever.

He got to his feet. 'You will need to pack your belongings and sell the furniture or give it to charity. I will arrange to have your things moved on Saturday.'

'Saturday?'

'There is no point in hanging around here. By the way, you will need to hand in your notice at work.'

'That's crazy. How will I survive?'

'My dear Magda, from now on you have no need to worry about work, money, bills or anything else.'

'Everything is happening so fast. I love my job at Simpsons.'

'It's your choice, my beautiful girl.'

She loved Rufus, so much, and she would grasp this opportunity of a new start with the man of her dreams.

'You're right. Let's do this.'

'One more thing – don't tell anyone your new address.'

'What about Emma?'

He turned and looked at her very seriously. 'Especially Emma. If this is to work between us, we will both have to make sacrifices. This is a new start for both of us. You have to let go of your past life.'

'Are you saying I mustn't see or speak to Emma again?'

'I am afraid that's the way it has to be; she and her family are in daily contact with people who know me. It would be impossible for you not to slip up and say something that would link us together. If you need time to absorb and consider moving into the apartment, that's fine. I don't want to force you to make decisions you're not ready to make. I will ring you on Thursday. That gives you two days to decide what you want to do.'

She had never contemplated life without Emma. They had become like sisters – she was the best friend Magda had ever had. The Fairchilds had opened their home to her, involved her in family life and all their social occasions. They had taught her so much.

Alas, life goes on. Emma would meet someone sooner or later, and then she would understand.

CHAPTER TEN

At ten o'clock on Saturday morning the removal van arrived dot on time. Magda's entire life had been boxed up and was ready to go. She had been in a total frenzy as there had been so much to do. The hardest thing had been keeping Emma away from visiting the flat and avoiding her invites out while trying to sound perfectly normal when she was bursting with excitement. The deadline to be packed and out of the apartment within two days enabled her to focus. No time to feel guilty.

She threw out most of her stuff, including half of her wardrobe and all the cheap paintings and ornaments picked up at street markets. She wanted to leave behind who she had been; this was a new chapter and she wanted to reinvent herself as part of a couple.

Saturday evening, alone in her new apartment, was like being in a dream. She loved the place and had to pinch herself to believe that she was actually going to be living there. Never would she have ever imagined the recent changes that had occurred in her life. Rufus was joining her the following morning. He was working at his apartment this evening.

'Darling, did everything go okay with the move?'

'Yes.'

'Are you settling in okay?'

'Oh, yes, it's a fabulous apartment.'

'No regrets?'

'None whatsoever.'

'I will have to get on with work and I'll see you around ten o'clock tomorrow morning. Goodnight, darling.'

'Goodnight, Rufus.'

Magda was upbeat. She had walked away from her old life and was ready to embrace a new life with the man of her dreams.

Rufus arrived at Magda's apartment. He pressed the intercom as he was unable to reach his keys. In one hand he had a floral bouquet of pink and white roses, in the other a bottle of champagne and under his arm a large box of continental chocolates. She rushed to meet him at the door.

'I know my gifts are conventional but that's the type of man I am.'

He smiled, dumping everything in the kitchen.

'Get two champagne glasses, darling.'

She put the glasses on the table and smiled. Rufus adored her youthful enthusiasm. He pulled her close to him. She was barely wearing any make-up – her complexion was fresh and radiant, her big brown eyes framed by long black lashes. He kissed her full lips, pillows of softness. Again, he thought how innocent and clean she was, untarnished by life and its trappings.

They held each other closely, her body was supple and slender. His hands smoothed over the apple curves of her bottom. He held her tightly and she caught her breath.

Lightening his grip and stroking her face gently, he whispered, 'I love you.'

Magda's smile widened. 'I love you too.'

Then, changing the mood, he announced, 'Champagne.'

The cork flew across the room.

She said, 'I'm going to keep this forever.'

'What? The cork? But why?'

'I want to.'

'There will be many more champagne corks, many more happy times.'

'But they will be different corks and different happy experiences.'

He shrugged his shoulders and handed her a flute of champagne.

'To us.' They toasted themselves.

The rest of the day and evening was spent as a proper couple. They cooked dinner together and talked and laughed. It was perfect.

'It would be nice to get away for a week, away from this weather.'

'Really? Where would we go?'

'I know someone with a place in Marbella, Spain. A beautiful villa with its own pool a few rows back from the coast, not far from bars and restaurants. We wouldn't see anyone who knew me – I wouldn't think it would be their cup of tea, but ideal for us.'

'It sounds wonderful.'

'I'll make the arrangements.'

'When will we go?'

'I have a break coming up in about three weeks' time?'

'Oh, but how will you explain …' She faltered.

'That's my problem. You think about getting your bikinis and sundresses.'

Her face was aglow. Things seemed to get better and better.

CHAPTER ELEVEN

Rufus looked out of his study window and saw Daphne with her two Yorkshire terriers, Popsy and Jolly, returning from a walk around the grounds. He loved Daphne dearly, and he went outside to join her. The dogs ran into the kitchen where Mrs Ronson would feed them. He wrapped his arm around Daphne's shoulder and she rested her head against his chest as they strolled slowly in the cool breeze.

Daphne said, 'Darling, you look sad.'

'No, not really. Well, I have to go away for a week or so,' he answered uncomfortably.

'Away. When and where are you going this time?'

'In three weeks, an important visit.'

'Excuse me, Lady Holroyd,' George, from the stables, called out. He waved for her to join him.

'Sorry, darling, I had better check in with George and see what he wants.'

'You go and speak to George. I'll see you later.' Relieved, he watched her walk away. He hated lying to her but he wanted to be with Magda so much he couldn't help himself.

Flying out with a budget airline, he was confident no one he knew would be on their flight, not to the Costa del Sol.

They took a taxi from the airport to Marbella. The journey was fraught, the road was hectic. The taxi drove through Marbella town and after a couple of right turns, set back from the coast, the pace of life suddenly slowed down.

Rufus had the remote key to open the large white gates at the villa. They drove onto the driveway and the bags were unloaded; they had arrived. It was amazing – a large, exquisite white-walled villa. Magda had never seen anything so wonderful. The interior was immaculate, stylish, and had clearly been professionally designed; the garden and pool area were pure bliss. Magda was enjoying letting life happen. They were in their own little world for the next week.

After she had unpacked and taken a shower she changed into a cool, cotton maxi dress. Outside, Rufus was as she had never seen him before, casually dressed in knee-length shorts, tee shirt and sandals. They had a perfect view of the sea, as the villa was quite high up. The breeze sent Magda's hair cascading across her face. Rufus couldn't take his eyes off her, she was so beautiful. Only God above knew how much he had fallen in love with her; he adored and desired her. Since he had met her, his life had taken on a new dimension. He was experiencing feelings he hadn't experienced for years; he felt young and that anything was possible.

Magda was taking in the view. 'It's beautiful, Rufus,' she said quietly.

Essentials had been placed in the fridge, ready for their arrival, by Antonia, the woman responsible for maintaining and cleaning the villa. Rufus set out the table and had made a green salad to go with a bottle of chilled white wine.

'Let's toast our future.'

'To us.' He kissed her.

The hours drifted by, and as the day closed in the night sky followed. The clear sky became filled with stars.

'Why can't we see the stars at home?'

'A number of reasons, the typical British clouds and light pollution.'

'What is that?'

'The lights from the cities and towns, exhaust fumes produce a haze which reduces our ability to see the stars, and of course pollution from industry.'

'Really?'

'Well, look around you, there is only the light from Marbella town.'

It was a still, warm night. Rufus took Magda's hand. 'Happy?'

'Yes, very happy.'

Rufus's light tan was getting deeper, his moustache and beard had lightened and the spray of grey in his hair was turning white. Magda wore her cut-off denims and a bikini top. More often than not she carried her sandals, happy to walk barefoot on the warm ground. During the day they chilled together by the villa's pool, read, swam, and walked to the local shops. Most evenings, they took a taxi to Puerto Banús. Magda loved the upmarket shops and trendy bars and restaurants. The boats at the port were magnificent and the cars that cruised by were Ferraris and Porsches. It was glitzy and glamourous; Magda loved this new opulent lifestyle.

'Magda, I want you to go into the boutiques, choose whatever dresses, tops, sandals you like and then give me a wave and I will come and pay for them.'

'Where will you be?'

'Sat on the wall, over there, in the sun.'

Magda entered a boutique and the sales assistant came over to her. 'Buenos dias, senora, English?'

'Yes.'

Magda selected a couple of dresses, skirts and halter neck tops.

'Let me take them for you, madam.' The sales lady took the items to the changing room. Magda followed.

'Excuse me, senora, I have two dresses newly arrived. They will look beautiful on your wonderful figure. May I get them for you to see?'

'Yes, please.'

She returned with two multi-coloured maxi dresses. 'They are new delivery.'

'They are gorgeous.' Magda tried them on. She stroked the material, it was so silky and expensive.

'Senora, you look amazing.'

'Would you do something for me?'

'Certainly.'

'My boyfriend is sat on the wall opposite the boutique, moustache, close-cut beard, would you give him a wave to join us.'

'Yes.'

Rufus followed the sales woman to the changing room.

'Senor, she looks beautiful, see.'

Rufus watched as Magda did a twirl in each dress; she was a picture of beauty. The dresses enhanced her fabulous figure and gave her an air of sophistication.

'Pass all the dresses and any other clothes you want to the sales lady. I will pay for them while you get dressed.'

'Thank you, I love you.' She blew him a kiss.

Magda was delighted to see the purchases had been packaged into three large, elegant boutique carriers.

'Thank you, darling.'

'You will look as expensive as the rest of the crowd.' He smiled.

She continued to see Rufus in a new light. He was so relaxed, informal and less intense. They didn't have to keep looking over their shoulders all the time, no sneaking around, no snatching precious time together. She had him all to herself.

They went to a favourite pasta restaurant, and both chose the seafood dish.

'We are like a proper couple.'

'We are a proper couple.'

'You know what I mean. We can be seen out together and talk to other couples. We don't have to watch what we say or keep a lookout for anyone you might know.'

'Yes, great, isn't it?'

'This is the best holiday ever.'

'There will be others, whenever I can get away.'

Magda savoured every minute of their last day on holiday. They sunbathed together by the pool, holding hands. Magic moments.

In the evening they strolled along an empty beach, gazed at the stars one last time, with the sound of the sea lapping upon the shore.

CHAPTER TWELVE

Being back in London was such an anti-climax. They had hit the ground running.

Magda was back at the Chelsea apartment and Rufus had returned to work. The coming weekend he would spend at Grange Manor.

Magda was in turmoil. Once more, Daphne's existence was a reality. He had a wife. Why wouldn't she set him free? Could she not accept she was no longer enough for him?

Feeling the loneliness begin to creep back, this time worse than before, she had nowhere to go, no friend to visit, no one to call or to talk to, no one to share the details of the fabulous holiday with.

To blot out the loneliness she opened a bottle of wine. A couple of glasses helped to dampen her frustration.

Daphne, believing he had been on an official visit to Italy, didn't ask much about his trip. She never asked too many questions regarding his travels that were work related; he would tell her if there had been anything on the agenda that was of interest to her. She was so glad to have him home, if only for the weekend.

'Darling, you're so tanned – the trip agreed with you, even though you have been working. I'm envious. We must get away on holiday together soon.'

'No need to be envious, dear, the trip was business. I have been very busy.'

'I know, but it would be nice to spend some time together in the sun.'

'Yes, you're right. I can't promise anything just yet.'

'I know that you are busy, darling. Anyway, I am happy at home. It was just a suggestion.'

Rufus, feeling terribly guilty, added, 'We will go somewhere as soon as I can clear some space in my diary, I promise.'

He went to his study, his solace. After reflecting on his lies and his infidelity, he got down to work dealing with constituents' correspondence. This helped him settle back into life at home.

At eight thirty, he and Daphne dined.

'I have so much to tell you, darling. The stables have been busy; George has taken on a new stable boy. Popsy and Jolly have had their annual boosters – they came home feeling very sorry for themselves.'

Rufus always tried to appear interested, her mundane chatter deflected from his lies about the trip to Italy. He was able to tell her about some of the concerns of his constituents. Daphne was particularly interested in letters concerning the conservation of the green belt areas.

After dinner, Rufus poured them both a large brandy. They took their drinks to the sofa, cuddled up and listened to their favourite classical music.

'It's always good to have you home.'

'It's always heaven to be home and to be with you.'

Rufus was speaking from the heart, meaning every word. His life in London was forgotten.

CHAPTER THIRTEEN

Two years had passed since Magda made her choice. During this time, she had pangs of guilt for dropping her friend Emma. Three letters had been forwarded to Magda's new address. Magda had written only one reply, telling Emma that she had moved on and was making a fresh start with the man in her life. She was relieved when Emma's letters ceased to arrive. Rufus was her priority now and he was all that she cared about.

Having quickly adjusted to her new privileged lifestyle, she was able to lie in every morning. Rufus called her numerous times a day and was able to stay over at least three nights a week. It was like one long honeymoon. He was so generous and so passionate.

Her world was very small. It was the apartment, shopping and Rufus.

By the third year something changed, they changed. Her easy lifestyle was the norm, and Magda started to want more. She wanted some form of commitment from Rufus. She had always imagined that things would evolve and that by now he would be with her every day; she simply hadn't considered that the arrangement would still be the same almost three years on.

With age comes assertiveness and she didn't shrink from making her feelings known to Rufus. He was spending more time at Grange Manor, which brought home the reality of Daphne's existence. This antagonised her even more. Rufus appeared to be less charmed by her; he had become far more dismissive and frequently abrupt. He was failing to make her feel special. She felt she was expected to earn his favour, which annoyed her intensely. They were growing apart. Magda knew what she wanted, she always had. It was Rufus who appeared to be getting more cautious about everything.

'Please, sit down, this apartment is your home as much as mine. Rufus, you used to stay over at least three nights a week. I'm lucky if you stay one night these days.'

'I have work commitments. I work into the night. I would never be able to knuckle down to it here, you'd be too much of a distraction.'

'Must you work every night?'

'At the moment, yes. I don't have a choice in what comes my way, I simply have to deal with it. I am a politician.'

'Why don't you give me your telephone number at the flat? At least I could call you in the evening.'

'I call you.'

'Sometimes you do, sometimes you don't.'

'I can't have you ringing me at all hours. I am either working or sleeping.'

'How long will these working evenings go on for?'

'How long is a piece of string?'

'I want you to stay over more often. I'm going stir crazy here all by myself.'

'Get out and do something. You're young, do whatever young people do.'

'I want to do things with you.'

'We will do things, but right now it's out of the question. I don't have a nine-to-five job. You know how difficult it is for me.'

'As long as this isn't forever.'

'No. It's just a demanding time.'

She would have to accept the situation for now. At least they were still together.

CHAPTER FOURTEEN

Rufus continued to split his time between Grange Manor, his apartment in central London and Magda's place in Chelsea. He was, however, spending less time with Magda. He always had some excuse – work commitments, meetings.

To save Magda from terminal boredom he had considered getting her a membership at the Chelsea health club but then decided it was too close to home. So, he arranged for her to spend as much time as she liked at the Lakeside health spa out in the countryside. Magda didn't know whether to accept it as a gift or an insult. Everything he did began to irritate her; she simply wasn't getting what she wanted anymore and she certainly expected an awful lot more than he had originally agreed he would provide. After all, she had invested three years of her life in this relationship. Disenchanted with everything, she wanted more but was getting less – certainly less time with Rufus. Some weeks he didn't stay over at all. Fewer phone calls, no explanation of his whereabouts. All was not well. She resented and despised Daphne and often wished Daphne were dead; but for that woman, they would be together.

Eight o'clock he had said; it was now nine thirty.

'Damn you, Rufus,' she yelled as she sat back heavily on the sofa, arms folded in defiance.

Hearing the key in the door, she sat silently and turned her head towards the window.

'Don't I even get a hello?'

'Damn you. Damn you, damn you.'

'What the hell?'

'I'll tell you what the hell. I have been waiting ninety minutes for you to make an appearance. Eight o'clock you said, well, didn't you? I am always last on the list these days. You don't even think to call to say you're going to be late.'

'Magda, calm down and let me explain.'

'Don't tell me to calm down, stop patronising me. I am sure you always remember to call dear old Daphne with some lame excuse as to why you'll be late. Well, don't you?'

'Shut up.'

'What?'

'Just shut up. I am sick and tired of your constant complaints. I am a member of parliament, for goodness' sake. I have responsibilities. I cannot skip important meetings, I cannot guarantee a meeting will not go on a lot longer than anticipated. Wake up, woman.'

'How dare you speak to me like that! Would you speak to Daphne in that manner?'

Rufus became very angry. His face turned red and he clenched his fists.

'I have never needed to speak to Daphne in that way because she understands the duties of a politician. Furthermore, I am sick of hearing you go on and on about Daphne. Stop bringing her into any disagreements we may have.'

'I can't help it – you appear to be more loyal to her.'

'She is my wife.'

'Oh, she's your wife, well thank you for the reminder, it makes me feel so much better.' Full of rage, she rushed to the kitchen. 'You bastard.'

'Why are you being so vile?'

The smashing of crockery echoed throughout the apartment, then silence.

He found Magda crouching on the floor; her hand was bleeding.

'For goodness' sake, what have you done?'

He threw off his overcoat and moved swiftly towards her, pulled her to her feet and towards the sink. She put her hand under the cold-water tap. It bled for some time. Although it was a deep cut, Rufus was relieved it hadn't been her wrist – that would have required hospital treatment and the last thing he needed was to be seen with a woman with a bleeding wrist in the casualty department. He went to the bathroom cabinet to look for plasters and bandages and was shocked to see it was cluttered with bottles of various medications. He found the bandages and went back to the kitchen. The bleeding had lessened. Magda was sitting at the kitchen table, subdued. She watched as he carefully bandaged her hand.

Tears began to roll down her face, like she was a vulnerable child needing someone to take care of her. Rufus began to mellow; his anger passed. He looked at her and smiled, then he picked her up and carried her to the sofa. He poured her a whisky to calm her. He knew that he had been in some way responsible for her hysterical outburst. He held her gently in his arms until she fell asleep.

Rufus had seen Magda frustrated and moody many times over the last year or two, but had never seen her behave the way she had this evening. On reflection, he realised she had been verging on hysteria a couple of times in the recent past, which he had managed to quell. He recalled that she had cut herself a number of times and had said it was an accident; perhaps it was. Things could never be the way Magda wanted them to be – he knew in his heart that he would never leave Daphne. Daphne was his foundation, his strength without whom he would crumble. The years he had spent with his wife counted for far more than could be seen on the surface. Daphne was more than his wife; she was his soulmate and that encompassed many roles. Magda was his lover and friend; she was the one with whom he recaptured his youth and vitality. He watched Magda as she slept. She looked so young. He felt a deep sense of sorrow as he could give her no more than he already had. He knew he should end their relationship before things got worse for Magda. He didn't want her to hurt anymore. Soon he would end their relationship, but for now he was letting his desire for Magda blur his better judgement.

Magda woke up and saw Rufus stretched out asleep on the floor by the fire. He had kicked off his shoes and had been looking through her magazine. Tears filled her eyes. She loved him so much; she decided she would try harder to make him happy. She would never leave him because one day they would be together.

'Ruffy,' she called in a tiny voice.

'Magda darling, how are you feeling?'

'Much better. I'm sorry I behaved the way I did. I love you. Do you still love me?'

'Yes, I still love you and I am sorry too. I should have got a message to you that I was going to be late. It really isn't that easy. It's imperative that you remain anonymous.'

'I guess so. *For now?*'

'I think you need cheering up. How about a short holiday?'

'Oh yes, when?'

'Leave it with me. I will work something out.'

Magda looked into his eyes and her heart dipped. She wouldn't worry about his timekeeping nor would she ever allow herself to get so upset and irrational again. After all, Ruffy loved her and only her.

* * *

Magda had managed to contain any further emotional outbursts, although it was not easy. She tolerated Rufus's continuous evasiveness regarding his whereabouts; he would only say that he had extremely important matters to deal with. One would think he was part of the secret service. He had made a few fleeting visits but hadn't mentioned the holiday he was supposed to be arranging. Magda had called the number to Rufus's office many times and then had put down the receiver. She had promised not to jeopardise their arrangement; there must not be any scandal.

But the strain of being the other woman, anonymous in the life of the man she loved, was taking its toll. It made her feel like a non-person. She didn't exist in Rufus's world and she no longer had a world of her own. Too much time spent alone caused her to be tense and anxious. No longer able to integrate with the rest of society she became an observer, unable to participate. She continued to find solace in alcohol; it numbed her senses and knocked her out each evening until the following morning. Like a mantra, she chanted, 'I must hang on.' They would be together. They had come this far.

* * *

At eight o'clock on a Tuesday evening she was awoken from her alcohol-induced slumber by the sound of the door closing. She rubbed her eyes and, smoothing down her big baggy jumper, she swiftly kicked the whisky bottle and glass under the sofa.

The door opened and a rush of cold air accompanied Rufus into the room.

'Darling, I didn't expect you today.' Standing up, unsteady on her feet, she greeted him. Small and insignificant, she was ashamed.

'You're looking rather dishevelled – have you been out today?'

'No. I've been nowhere for a couple of days. I waited at home in case you called.'

'You shouldn't sit around waiting for me to call. Get out there and do something.'

'Like what?' she snapped.

'How should I know? Am I expected to arrange your leisure time too? Why not go to Lakeside Spa? It's all arranged for you, you can go whenever you like. Give them a call and go tomorrow, get yourself together. I am disappointed to see you like this.'

'You're right. I need to get out.'

Rufus strolled into the kitchen and returned with two cups of coffee. She was on the sofa; he sat adjacent on the chair. He looked around the room and then at Magda and sighed. The lounge was untidy; in fact, it was a mess, clothes strewn everywhere, cups and plates left on the floor.

She felt unattractive and uneasy, knowing she had disappointed him.

'I only have a couple of hours to spare. Why don't you take a shower and tidy yourself up? We could go for a walk?'

'No, I'm not in the mood to go out now.'

'I have to be back at the Commons in a couple of hours and it is imperative that I speak with you.'

'You make it sound terribly serious.'

'It is. I should have told you some time ago, but I didn't want to concern you unnecessarily.'

'Tell me what?'

He took a deep breath. 'I have put myself forward to be a member of the European Parliament.'

'Why?'

'I think it is the right thing for me to do.'

'Please don't become hysterical.'

'But you said you would be standing down next time.'

'Yes, stand down from my current position as member of parliament.'

'You said that would be it. No more politics, more time for us to be together.'

She noticed how he fidgeted, twisted his hands and looked away from her.

'Yes, I admit I may have given you that impression but—'

'Given me the impression? You said it, no more politics.'

'Now hold on. I said nothing specific. I was toying with the idea – it seemed an attractive option at the time. But on reflection …'

'Oh, on reflection, on reflection, am I not to be consulted in these life-changing decisions? We have been together for three years. Are you tiring of me, am I not as appealing as I once was? Has the novelty worn off?'

Rufus remained silent.

'You owe me.'

'I owe you nothing. Hear me, nothing. I don't have to explain myself to you.'

'I gave up my job, my friends, everything to be with you.'

'No one held a gun to your head. You knew the set-up and you walked into it with your eyes open.'

'Because I love you. You're the most important thing in my life, I live for you. Does that not count for anything?'

'Of course, but I too have made sacrifices.'

'What have you sacrificed?'

'Do you think I enjoy lying to my wife?'

Magda's heart thumped against her chest. 'Don't do this. Don't bloody well bring her into this conversation.'

'I have to – she is my wife. I have an obligation to her.'

'What about your obligation to me?'

'I have always tried to consider you, but it isn't easy.'

'It could be. Leave her, why can't you just leave her? Let her keep Grange Manor. She will have lots of money and security.'

'No, it doesn't work that way.'

'Don't you love me anymore?'

'I do.'

'Tell me, say it, tell me that you love me.'

Rufus raised his hand to his head. 'For goodness' sake, Magda.'

'Say it!'

'I love you. I care about you, but life goes on. I cannot abandon my responsibilities and commitments in the name of love.'

'You mean you can't for me.'

He stared at the floor and then looked up. 'I simply cannot give you what you want at this point in time. Perhaps you should get out now and meet someone your own age.'

Magda was horrified at the thought of not seeing him again; she couldn't live without him. Maybe if she hung on a little longer, if she was a little more patient, she would win him over to her way of thinking.

'Rufus, forget what I just said. Maybe I am being selfish. I know it isn't easy for you. Let's forget it. Why don't you finish off what you came here to tell me?'

Rufus's expression was one of relief; he didn't hesitate in dropping the subject.

'I tried to explain earlier. I have put myself forward as a prospective member of the European Parliament. I feel confident I will be elected and this will change things drastically.'

'What does that mean? Will I see even less of you?'

'I'm afraid that's exactly what it means. To be ruthlessly honest I will be in Brussels most of the time.'

'Brussels? For fuck's sake.'

'Brussels is where the job is.'

'Will I be able to visit you?'

'That would be out of the question.' He gazed out of the window.

'Why? I could pretend to be a tourist. We could meet in secret. It would be exciting – I have never been to Brussels.'

There was a pause.

'Daphne is coming with me.'

She was unable to take in what he had just said. 'She will be visiting you?'

'Daphne will be with me most of the time.'

Magda got to her feet and began to pace up and down. 'Is that what you want?'

'It is no longer a case of what I want. This is the way it has to be.'

'You have engineered this to be rid of me.'

'Don't flatter yourself. I wouldn't uproot myself and move to another country just to be rid of you. Give me some credit.'

'So, you don't want to be rid of me?'

'Magda, please.'

'How am I supposed to manage without you? When will I see you?'

'We will sort something out. In the meantime, you should smarten yourself up. Get out more. After all, I want my Magda to be radiant when I see her.'

She was relieved that he would continue to see her.

'I must be going.' He stood up and began to walk towards the door.

'When will I see you again?'

'Soon. I will drop by next week after a decision has been made about my political future.'

He kissed her on the cheek. She flung her arms around him and held on to him.

'I must go.' Once free from her embrace, he left the room.

'I love you,' she called.

'Oh yes, love you.'

Shell-shocked, she had to face the fact they wouldn't be together much for the next few years. What scared her was not knowing how much longer she could cope. She needed to get her act together. She showered, put a colour on her hair, used a face mask to help her skin glow, gave herself a manicure. After taking a sleeping tablet, she went to bed, but four hours later she was still awake, so she took another pill.

CHAPTER FIFTEEN

One week later.

'Hello. Grange Manor, how may I help you?'

'Mrs Ronson, Sir Rufus here, I need to speak with Lady Holroyd.'

'Of course, sir.'

There was a pause.

'Hello, Rufus.'

'Darling, I wanted to tell you personally before you heard it elsewhere …'

'Let me guess, you are now a member of the European Parliament?'

'Correct.'

'Congratulations, darling. I am absolutely thrilled. What time will you be home?'

'I intend to go to the club, first, but if you would prefer me to come home …?'

'Yes, Rufus. We could celebrate, just the two of us.'

'That sounds perfect, although I will drop in at the club. They will be expecting me after this good news – just for an hour and then I will leave London and make haste to be with the woman I love.'

'Splendid, we will have the whole weekend together.'

'Bye, Daphne, I love you.'

'I love you too.'

At his club he was joined by well-wishers who delighted in celebrating his good news with champagne. Rufus slipped away to make a private call.

'Magda, it's me.'

'Hi.'

'I am at the club so I can't speak for long. I wanted to tell you the news personally. I am a member of the European Parliament.'

'Congratulations.'

'Thank you. I need to go home for the weekend. I have a lot to sort out. I will call you next week.'

'Okay. But when will I see you?'

'Soon. You can imagine this is going to change things. I must go, bye.'

'Bye, Rufus.'

Rufus loved to return to his country home away from professional and personal problems and demands. During the drive along those country lanes, London ceased to exist. The large electronic gates opened and he drove up the long driveway that was lined on both sides with large oak trees. The leaves fluttered onto the gravel driveway. A lamp above the main doorway to Grange Manor gave off a warm, orange glow.

Daphne greeted him as he pulled up by the main entrance. He cherished the predictability of life at Grange Manor;

each time he arrived home it was as if time had stood still – Daphne always there, loving and understanding, the loyal staff team who were totally dependable. He hoped Brussels wouldn't be too much of an upheaval for Daphne now she had at last found peace of mind.

'Darling, you're home earlier than I expected.' Her face was alight with joy.

'Shall I go away and come back again later?'

'Don't be silly.' She hugged him tightly. 'I am so excited about moving to Brussels. We will be able to spend so much more time together.'

'Wow, slow down.'

'I can't help it. I know it's going to be marvellous.'

Daphne, took his arm and they walked into the drawing room.

Rufus went to the drinks cabinet and poured himself a whisky on ice.

'Won't you miss Grange Manor?'

'Yes, I shall, but the bonus will be spending time with you, living together day in, day out.'

'I will be busy all day, dear, I will have to put in the hours.'

'The difference is every evening you will return home to me. You are the most important person in my life.'

'How will you spend your days?'

'There will be plenty for me to do. I will get involved in charitable or voluntary work. Also, Popsy and Jolly will be with me.'

'Speaking of important things in your life, what arrangements will you make regarding staff and stables?'

'Mrs Ronson will stay on as housekeeper and Jenny and Claire will continue with cleaning duties. George will continue to run the stables with the stable boys. It will more or less remain the same here.'

'You have it all in hand. I need to go to my study; there is something that needs my attention and it won't wait.'

'How long will it take?'

'A couple of hours or so.'

'Mrs Ronson has prepared a celebratory meal. Shall I tell her we will dine late, around 10.30 p.m.?'

'Er, yes okay.'

The prospect of the move to Brussels had invigorated Daphne; he hoped it would live up to her expectations.

'Cedric, Rufus here, sorry to ring so late but I wondered if I could run something by you?'

'Of course. Congratulations on becoming a member of the European Parliament.'

'Thank you. I am worried about Daphne. She is over the moon about the move to Brussels and I am glad of that, but she seems elated. The medication has kept her calm and rational for a number of years – I wonder if she might have stopped taking her tablets or if she thinks Brussels is the holy grail.'

'Perhaps it's neither and she is simply ready to move on.'

'Should I suggest we make an appointment with Dr Robinson, have a consultation before all the change?'

'Discuss it with Daphne. It sounds like a good idea and it will put your mind at rest.'

'Thank you, Cedric. I will catch up with you soon.'

Rufus sat at his desk and looked around the study that had been his solace for so many years. He was apprehensive about his new position in Brussels but he needed change, he needed to get away.

'Darling, you've finished already? I'll tell Mrs Ronson, we will dine straight away. She will be delighted as she thought the meal would have dried out within the next hour.'

After dinner, Rufus decided to deal with his concerns.

'Daphne, I am pleased that you are so positive about the move to Brussels. I wondered if we should make an appointment with Dr Robinson, before we go. It's a big change for you and I wouldn't want you to get there and become overwhelmed.'

'Do you think I might relapse?'

'No, I just think it would be reassuring to get his perspective on the matter.'

'Okay, that is very thoughtful of you, darling.'

Rufus had always taken care of Daphne; he protected and shielded her wherever possible. He never burdened her with his problems or worries. However, he had been unable to protect her from the devastation of two miscarriages and then being told she would never be able to have children. Maybe she wasn't fragile anymore.

'Darling, just one more call to make, then I am all yours.'

'Magda. It's me.'

'Hi, I was still up. I am glad you called.'

'We need to end our relationship.'

'What? Where has this come from? I thought we had resolved this.'

'I have always been honest with you. This was never going to last forever. I want what is best for you and this isn't it.'

'What is best for me or what is best for you?'

'I will always care for you and I won't leave you high and dry. Stay at the apartment for another year, I will honour our arrangement until you find work. You need to start making a life for yourself. Do you understand? You have your whole life ahead of you.'

'We can't just end it, like it means nothing.'

'We must. I need you to promise not to tell anyone about us. Are you still there?'

The line went dead.

What the hell had he done? Daphne must never know of his affair; her wellbeing was his priority.

That night he made love to his wife, but he felt he was betraying Magda.

The next day, he and Daphne went riding across their many acres of land. It had been a long time since they had been so close, safe and secure together. It reminded him of when he first brought Daphne home to meet his parents.

Daphne and Rufus invited some friends over for dinner: Cedric and his wife, Penny, and Jason and Claire Roxton.

'We shall miss you both once you have relocated to Brussels,' Cedric lamented.

'Indeed, we will,' agreed Penny.

'We intend to come home as often as possible, don't we, Rufus?'

'Yes, who knows, we might see even more of each other than we do now.'

'When do you go? Perhaps I could come with you – I don't think Cedric would miss me.'

'Well maybe not at first.'

They all laughed.

'No set date as yet. It will all happen pretty soon.'

'What about Grange Manor?'

'The staff will carry on as normal.'

'Who will be in charge? What if the staff have wild parties?'

'I assure you none of our staff are hell raisers and Mrs Ronson will be in charge. Nothing will get past Mrs R.'

'I wonder, Cedric, if you would kindly be a port of call should any problems arise?'

'Rufus, no problem, you can rely on me.'

Claire Roxton waited for a lull in conversation and then asked, 'Daphne, did you ever go to stay with Rufus in London?'

'No. I have too much to do here.'

'Not good for a man to spend so much time alone away from home.'

'Well, that won't be a problem for much longer.'

'What about the place in Chelsea – will you keep it?'

'I beg your pardon?' Rufus began to panic.

Daphne was completely bewildered. 'No, Claire, we don't have a place in Chelsea. Rufus is at the Barbican.'

'Sorry, someone, can't for the life of me remember who, said you had a place in Chelsea. Rufus has been seen in the area, restaurants and such.'

'Clearly, your source is mistaken.' His heart was thudding. 'Come to think of it, I have had a few meetings in Chelsea but it was some time ago.'

'Darling, you never mentioned it.'

'Just the occasional, boring, business meetings.'

'Perhaps your acquaintance mixed up Kensington with Chelsea; they are the same borough. Rufus and I have friends in South Kensington.'

Claire looked at her husband and raised an eyebrow. Cedric seemed interested in their exchange. But Daphne appeared oblivious to the dynamics of the group. The rest of the evening went smoothly, although Rufus never did regain his earlier relaxed composure. He was left with a queasy churning in the pit of his stomach. Who had seen him and where? He had been discreet. He had on occasion run into someone whom he was on nodding terms with, but no one of importance. He would have to appease Magda, for the next couple of weeks, after which he and Daphne would be in Brussels and then Magda would be out of his life forever.

CHAPTER SIXTEEN

On his return to London, Rufus had called Magda and arranged to see her.

Paranoid, he looked around as he locked the car and made his way into the apartment.

'Oh, it's so good to see you,' Magda said.

'Please don't fling yourself at me. I need to explain our predicament. Please sit down.'

'Okay.'

'I shall be leaving for Brussels at short notice.'

'Should that not be you and your wife will be leaving at short notice?'

'Don't start …'

'Perhaps I should visit you in Brussels?'

Rufus knew this was a veiled threat. 'Don't be ridiculous.'

'So, what's the alternative?'

'I told you before, we have to end it.'

'I'm not ready to be alone. Could we do this on a gradual basis? That's not much to ask after three years.'

He was losing his resolve, giving in yet again, scared of another tantrum. 'I suppose we might see each other, but not very often.'

'Fine!' Magda sat with her arms folded.

'I don't think it's wise for us to go out together again.'

'What? I feel like a prisoner. I must be the best kept secret in the world.'

'I know it isn't satisfactory, but we can't do anything that might provoke a scandal. We have been lucky so far. Your name is already known to my secretary due to your recent irrational calls.'

'I'm sorry about those calls.'

'Forget it. The main thing now is to keep everything low key. I understand if you want to walk away right now.'

'Rufus, I would never walk away from you. I want to spend as much time with you as you can give me.'

'But, as we need to bring our relationship to a close, I would understand you wanting to start a new life as soon as possible.'

'Are you staying over?'

'That's not a good idea.'

'Please, Rufus, you will be in Brussels soon and I will see less and less of you. Please stay, I need you to stay, I don't want another night alone.'

'Okay, but just tonight.'

Against his better judgement he decided it was time for damage limitation. He wished he were a million miles away.

'I'll order us a takeaway and there is a bottle of Chablis in the fridge,' Magda said, sounding delighted.

Opening a second bottle of wine, Rufus started to relax and resigned himself to being there; they became closer and she rested her head upon his shoulder.

Rufus had fallen asleep on the sofa. He drifted in and out of a dream. He was roused by Magda gently calling his name.

'Rufus, Rufus.'

He opened his eyes to behold a visual delight. She was wearing black, lacy underwear, the bra pushed her breasts high, their fullness emphasising deep cleavage. Black stockings held up by skimpy lace suspenders and four-inch stiletto heels. The heels were pencil thin. Poised, she looked down at him; she looked incredible. She knew what he liked. She had him.

For the next couple of weeks, Rufus made an effort to call Magda at least three times a week, visiting once a week. He had to keep her sweet.

She had become needy again. He didn't like that, and the threat of them being found out had diminished his libido. He spent weekends at Grange Manor where he tried to forget about the mess he had created.

His last week at Westminster was full of good wishes, cards and gifts. Rufus would miss the staff team, who were like family. He couldn't face Magda again. He took the cowardly way out and rang her with a feeble excuse that he had an emergency meeting. He knew he had to give her something in return; it would have to be a number he could be reached on, only in an emergency. It was a compromise he had to make, to ensure she didn't lapse into one of her self-destructive phases. Following the conversation and Magda's tearful goodbye, he set off on his journey home to Daphne.

'We are all set for the move to Brussels, only a day away.'

A call came for Rufus, from his secretary in London.

'I am so sorry to call you at home, Sir Rufus.' Mrs Kay was clearly embarrassed.

'Miss Magda Rainford has called the office numerous times this morning demanding to speak with you. I did try to explain that you could no longer be reached at Westminster but she said it was urgent.'

She was becoming a liability. What should he do?

'Thank you, Mrs Kay. Should she call again tell her you have passed on the message. I will deal with the matter.'

'Thank you, Sir Rufus.'

Daphne and Rufus held a farewell dinner party for their friends and a number of fellow members of parliament and their wives. Daphne had brought in outside caterers for the occasion. Waiters and waitresses had been hired to serve drinks and a five-course meal. It was a special occasion and everything had to be perfect. Daphne thoroughly enjoyed the evening in celebration of Rufus's success. Entertaining was something they had done little of over the past few years because of Rufus's unpredictable work schedule. She was warm and mellow from the three large glasses of red wine. Rufus, however, was preoccupied and relieved that Jason and Claire had not made any further mention of Chelsea. Their presence still made him feel uneasy. He began to think carefully about his predicament.

Later that evening, when everyone had retired to the drawing room, Rufus took his friend Cedric to one side and asked him to join him in his study. Once behind closed doors, Rufus took a deep breath.

'Cedric, I have done something very stupid. I need your help.'

Rufus told Cedric everything.

'Rufus, because my department works closely with the security service doesn't mean I can use them to assist in a cover up for my friend.'

'There must be something you can do? I am desperate. What will it do to Daphne?'

'I am not comfortable with this.'

'Could you help get rid of the paper trail that leads to me?'

'I need to think about this.'

'I took out the rental agreement under an alias.'

'You did what?'

'I know – it was utter madness.'

'Rufus, I have no intention of doing anything that is against the law. I will do what I can.'

CHAPTER SEVENTEEN

'Miss Rainford, I cannot prescribe you any more tranquilisers. You have had many months' supply of this medication and it is time to stop. I will prescribe you a short course of sleeping tablets to help you sleep.'

'Just one more week's supply of the diazepam. Please.'

'I will prescribe a course of ten of the diazepam tablets, one to be taken every other day. Let us see how you manage reducing them gradually. Come back and see me in two weeks' time.'

Magda had become bloated, her face and eyes puffy and her skin flaky with an unhealthy pallor. She knew she looked a mess and she was feeling dreadful.

In desperation she booked herself into Lakeside Spa. Rufus had paid in advance for a minimum of eight stays a year. He had been convinced it would help her both physically and psychologically. His idea had been that she would go there whenever she was at a loose end. Well, she had plenty of those now. The fees were extortionate but it ensured only elite clientele crossed the threshold.

Lakeside was able to accommodate her for a three-night stay. She packed a small holdall. She didn't need much; the spa provided most of what she needed.

From the train station she took a taxi to the spa. It was located in the middle of nowhere.

Once checked in, she was shown to her room, which was spacious and pleasant. She dumped her bag on the floor and, after taking a bottle of water from the mini bar, she lay back on the bed and read the spa menu. It offered a daily routine of prescriptive facials, massages, aromatherapy, reflexology ... the list was endless. She had packed her medication and a small bottle of whisky just in case she needed a drop.

It took the medication combined with the whisky to calm her and help her sleep, otherwise intense fear overwhelmed her and then the panic attacks would start. Her doctor had suggested Magda consider seeing a psychiatrist, but she had refused. She believed the symptoms would vanish when she and Rufus were together again, permanently, in a few years. She just had to sit it out until then.

She began to feel better as the day progressed. When she dined early at the spa restaurant, Magda's appetite returned and she realised how much she had been neglecting herself. She had been surviving on pills, booze and junk food.

The following morning, after breakfast, she took a swim then settled down on a lounger to read a book. It was tranquil and peaceful. She drifted in and out of sleep.

She rubbed her eyes and remembered where she was. She sighed, reassured in the knowledge she wasn't alone at the apartment.

Magda sensed someone close to her and, opening her eyes slowly and looking up, she saw a tall woman looking back at her. Magda rummaged around for her book and then pretended to read it.

Unable to fathom why this woman wouldn't take the hint and clear off, she asked, 'Hello, can I help you?'

'No, I'm sorry. I haven't got my spectacles with me, I thought you were someone else.'

'That's okay.' Returning to her book, she read the same line three times. The woman remained standing there. Magda looked up at her and smiled.

'Are you okay?'

'Yes, dear, thank you for asking. I am Rosalind Bartholomew, but people call me Ros. Pleased to meet you.'

'Likewise. I'm Magda Rainford.'

'What a charming name. Would you mind if I joined you?'

'Please do.' What else could she say?

'When did you arrive?'

'Yesterday.'

'Me too. Where do you travel from?'

'London.' Magda's eyes returned to the pages of her book.

'I rarely go to London now,' the woman said while continuing to stare at Magda.

'Where do you travel from?' Magda asked.

'I now live in a small village in Berkshire, you wouldn't know it, it's the sort of place one stumbles upon.'

'I have never been to Berkshire. I haven't been anywhere much in the UK.'

'What do you do in London?'

'I was a secretary but things changed and I'd rather not talk about it.'

'That's fine, dear.'

Magda let the woman drone on and on. Magda noted her heavily tanned complexion, steely blue eyes, and brassy blonde hair that poked out of her headwrap.

'Would you mind if I pull up this lounger next to yours?' Not waiting for a reply, she took off her robe and revealed her statuesque physique in a black and gold swimsuit.

Lying back on the lounger, she took out a cigarette, put it in a long cigarette holder and lit it.

'I don't think they allow smoking by the pool or anywhere inside the spa.'

'They don't mind me having the odd cigarette. People do occasionally complain but I am a regular here, so they bend the rules.'

The long black cigarette holder sat poised between her long fingers, finished with red talon-like nails.

Magda found herself enjoying the conversation; having someone to talk to was what she had missed.

'Tell me, dear, are you married or in a relationship?'

She was so desperate to talk about Rufus, the floodgates opened. 'I have been seeing a man I love dearly for three years. He is trying to cool things.'

'Cool things?'

'I think he wants to end our relationship. Actually, he told me he wants to end it.'

'What about you?'

'Gosh no, I think we can ride out the storm. I just have to hang in there, until he sees things the same as me.'

'My dear, I consider myself an expert regarding the male species. They fall into two categories: cads and bores. You have the former and I had the latter.'

Magda smiled. She hadn't spoken to anyone about her relationship before and Mrs Bartholomew seemed to be sympathetic to her situation.

'Are you married?'

'I am a widow.'

'Sorry.'

'Don't be. I have been widowed for a number of years. Over the years I considered dating, but I don't want their emotional baggage.' She paused. 'I suspect my husband had a mistress.'

'Why do you say that?'

'In truth, he was entitled to a lover. That side of our marriage never appealed to me. I think I have only ever loved one man.'

'Was he with someone else?'

Ros didn't answer.

'That's the situation I'm in. He's married and doesn't want to leave her.'

'They never do, dear. Do they have children? I don't mean to pry.'

'It's okay. No, they have no children.'

'How old is he?'

'Mid-forties.'

'Why is a young, attractive, intelligent woman waiting around for this man?'

'I love him. He is so handsome and clever. We have had some fabulous times together and super holidays.'

'Recently?'

'No.'

'I decided many years ago that love is for fools. A woman in love leaves herself open to be manipulated, and ends up emotionally battered and bruised. My definition of love is the using of one person by another.'

'It's not like that with us.'

'I'm sure it isn't.'

'Thanks for listening.'

'If you want to talk about anything at all, you can confide in me.'

'Thank you. Were you once hurt by someone you loved?'

Ros took a deep breath. 'Yes. Who hasn't been? But that was a lifetime ago.'

Magda was so pleased to have found someone to whom she could unburden herself.

'Shall we meet in the restaurant for dinner?'

'I would love to, Ros.'

It was great to have a friend at last. Magda was actually feeling happy and hopeful. This woman was older and wiser and understood matters of the heart.

Ros was already at the table when Magda arrived for dinner.

'I was thinking about your situation, dear. You really need a support network.'

'I have you, to talk to.'

'Chatting to me every blue moon isn't a support network. I really worry that you are so alone in the world.'

'That's kind of you. I appreciate your friendship.'

'My dear girl, someone so young, and with so much love to give, shouldn't be wasting it on a man who is married. A man who has no intention of leaving his wife. Why not get out into the world and meet someone new? You wouldn't need to tell the married chap. What's good for the goose, as they say.'

'I don't want anyone else. I could never feel the same about anyone else.'

'Maybe not, but this man will only cause you heartbreak.'

'Could we change the subject please? I hate to even contemplate not having my Rufus in my life.'

'Very well. Don't say I didn't try.'

CHAPTER EIGHTEEN

Magda returned home to find no messages on the answer machine. 'Damn him.'

On impulse, she rang the Brussels number he had given her.

'Sir Rufus is away at present and I cannot confirm the date of his return.'

What if he had instructed his secretary to say he was away? What if the bitch fancied her chances with her Rufus? Well, she would just have to keep ringing until he got the message that Magda Rainford was not about to fade into insignificance. She was here to stay.

After pouring herself a third whisky, she staggered slightly towards the television and switched it on. The evening news blurted out stories of doom and gloom. She was jolted from her tipsy state by footage of Rufus and Daphne leaving a conference in London.

'The bastard has been in London.' She hurled the glass at the television; it missed the screen. Her aim was as bad as her mood. The glass smashed against the wall. The whisky dribbled its way down to the carpet where it had already splashed and was soaking in. Dark brown stains. It looked disgusting.

131

Seeing Rufus and Daphne together troubled her deeply. He never used to speak of his wife or Grange Manor, but more recently he had repeatedly spoken of his other life, which greatly annoyed her. His lack of sensitivity made her feel betrayed. Whenever he used Daphne's name it was like a blow to the stomach, but seeing them together brought home the fact that it was she who was on the side line with no life of her own, living in Rufus's shadow. No one knew she existed. After three years, they had no mutual friends. How had she let this happen?

Ros had said she would be back at the spa in a couple of weeks. Magda grabbed the telephone.

'I would like to make a two-night reservation for the weekend of the 25th.'

'That is all booked in for you, Miss Rainford. We look forward to welcoming you back.'

It was reassuring that she would see her new confidante again very soon. She needed the support of a friend.

In the meantime, she needed to re-join the human race, and she decided she would draw up a daily routine, starting with a walk. She would shop for new clothes and visit the hairdressers. It was time to up her game.

Being at the spa gave her a sense of belonging, and although Rufus was always at the back of her mind, she was less tormented.

Coming out of the hot sauna and standing under the ice-cold shower sent shock waves through her emotionally bruised body, revitalising her. She put on her robe and went to lie on a lounger with a glass of fresh orange juice. Magda had decided she would have to assert herself to get what she wanted. She must become 'a force to be reckoned with'. That's what Ros had said.

'I must do whatever it takes.' She drifted into a peaceful sleep; she could always sleep when she was at the spa.

The following morning, at the buffet breakfast, Magda looked around to see if Ros was there. Taking a table by the window, she watched the other guests. Some were in couples or small groups of women on a short break, others were alone like her. The nice thing about being at the spa was that no one bothered you, nor was it seen as odd to be alone.

'Hello, Magda dearest. Lovely to see you again so soon.'

Magda's face lit up as Ros joined her.

'I remembered you saying you would be here this weekend, so I thought I would come myself.'

'How is that man friend of yours?'

That was Magda's cue to pour everything out. 'I haven't heard or seen anything of him. What makes it worse is that he has been in London and couldn't be bothered to leave a message.'

'I saw the bounder on the news. He was with his wife, wasn't he?' Ros watched Magda closely.

'Yes.'

'Things are not looking good.'

'I know they're not. I have got to do something, but what?'

'Start to build yourself a support network.' Ros moved forwards.

'I have you, you're a friend.'

'What did I tell you last time? Seeing me, on odd occasions, isn't support. Do you intend to let your man go or are you prepared to fight for him?'

'I will do whatever it takes to keep him.'

'See the woman over there? The dumpy one with short dark hair – she is a journalist. She writes for the *London Standard*. Why don't you get to know her?'

'Why?'

'Magda dear, you are in a long-term relationship with a prominent MEP. You have the power, not him. You have nothing to lose; he has everything to lose. Look at your situation. You are alone – no family, no friends, no job. He is all you have, and if he leaves you, you have nothing. Whereas he, on the other hand, has everything to lose, his marriage, his career and most of all his reputation.'

'What should I do?'

'Talk to the journalist, give her a few nuggets, tempt her with your information.'

'What would I say?'

'Start with small talk, say you might have a major scoop for her. You could tell her your name and drop a hint about your liaison with a member of parliament and bring Brussels into the mix. She would be on it like wild fire.'

'Do you think I should?'

'Think? Absolutely certain, trust me.'

'I do trust you. What if she isn't interested?'

'You are so naive. Of-course she'll be interested; it's dynamite.'

'I'll think it over.'

'Don't take too long. If you miss your chance to talk with her while she's here, that option will have passed you by, never to return.'

Magda was like a pendulum swinging from wishful thinking of wanting everything to work itself out to taking extreme action, but she couldn't deny how dire the situation was.

Pills, whisky and Ros were all she had. She needed more allies.

After agonising throughout the night, Magda decided to approach the journalist Rhiannon Roe.

'I'll do it. I will speak to the journalist.'

'Good for you. Take back the power.'

'Will you help me?'

'Yes, follow my lead.'

Choosing their moment, they walked over to where Rhiannon was sitting.

'What a dismal day it is. It makes you glad to be indoors.'

Rhiannon looked up at Rosalind, who was wearing a robe, headwrap and face mask. Ros nodded at Magda to follow her lead. She remembered Ros's advice. Start with small talk, introduce yourself, mention politics, slip in about man trouble and that he is married. Rhiannon had returned her attention to her magazine. Ros walked away while Magda sat on a chair opposite Rhiannon; leaning forwards, she spoke in a hushed tone.

'I know we haven't met before and it must seem strange that I am going to share with you my woes, but this man I have been in a relationship with for three years is a prominent figure in politics.'

'Really.' Rhiannon didn't bother to look up from her magazine.

'He is a married politician.'

'Which party?'

'Conservative.'

'The back-to-basics brigade.'

'He is now a member of the European Parliament, based in Brussels.'

Magda had said the magic words; that got her attention.

'Why should this interest me?'

'You're a journalist – you dig out the truth and expose the lies.'

'Who is he?'

She hesitated. She was about to open a can of worms. 'Sir Rufus Holroyd.'

Rhiannon looked at Magda, in disbelief as she considered what she had said. Is this the kind of woman Rufus Holroyd would shack up with for three years? She was young, attractive and intelligent. But she certainly wasn't intellectual or cultured.

But intellect and culture wouldn't be high on his list when partaking in his extra curriculum. Sir Rufus had a reputation for being loyal and dedicated to politics, he was in a long-term marriage, there had never been a whiff of scandal around him.

Rhiannon listened, noting that Magda was a troubled young woman. If or when this story blew it would be dynamite – a public scandal. She couldn't sit on this and let someone else expose the story. *Rhiannon Roe, this could be the making of you.*

'Let's meet up in the lounge in thirty minutes, we need a bit of privacy.'

Rhiannon, dressed in more formal attire, was waiting in a quiet area of the lounge. She had a recorder with her. Magda sat down opposite her.

After switching on the tape recorder, Rhiannon started to ask questions that Magda was ill-prepared for and her confidence began to wane.

'I want dates, times and places.'

Magda's head was foggy as she tried to put the past few years in order.

Thirty minutes later, a story was starting to form.

'Let me run through this with you. You first met Sir Rufus at a Conservative Party dinner dance, where he was the guest speaker?'

'Yes.'

'Remind me how you came to be there?'

'As a guest of Charles Fairchild MP and his family. I am— was a close friend of his daughter, Emma.'

'Would they back up your account?'

'Yes, but surely you won't need to involve them.'

Magda was uncomfortable, the situation was spiralling out her of control.

'Moving on. When did you next have contact with Sir Rufus?'

'He invited me to the Houses of Parliament. He took me on a tour of the building. We had tea and biscuits, after which I was going to leave but he invited me to dinner.'

'Just go back a step. He invited you, via the Fairchild's or directly?'

'Directly. A letter arrived on Houses of Parliament stationery. The Fairchild's knew nothing about our relationship. They still don't.'

'Where did you dine?'

'The little Italian restaurant in the centre of Covent Garden.'

'What happened next?'

'We had a pleasant evening. We exchanged telephone numbers.'

'His home phone number or his flat in London?'

'Neither. The number was to his office.'

'At the Houses of Parliament?'

'Yes.'

'So, at this point it was still a fledgling friendship?'

'Yes, I wasn't sure what to make of it. I just knew I liked him and he appeared to like me too.'

'Carry on.'

'We started meeting for lunch or for a walk at lunchtime, always around Covent Garden. It was our place.'

'Very sweet. Continue.'

'We got to know each other better; he asked to take me out for dinner.'

'Where?'

'We dined at a restaurant in Chelsea.'

'Why Chelsea?'

'I guess his friends didn't live in Chelsea. I really don't know for sure. A few months on he surprised me with my own apartment in Chelsea.'

'Is the apartment in your name?'

'No. It's rented.'

'You have been living there for three years?'

'Yes.'

'Does he stay over?'

'He used to stay up to three nights a week, but that stopped some months ago.'

'Why do you think that is?'

'Pressure.'

'What pressure?'

'He said he found it stressful living a double life. He didn't like lying to his wife.'

'After three years?'

'He said we should end our relationship. It would be for the best.'

'Do you agree?'

'No, we have weathered the storm before.'

'Going back to the exchanging of telephone numbers. I assume at some point he gave you the number to his London flat?'

'No.'

'Don't you find that odd?'

'Yes, I have asked many times. He said he will call me. That I would interrupt his work. He works at his flat in the evenings.'

'Do you believe him?'

'Yes.'

'Anything else you can think of?'

'We had a few holidays abroad, Spain, Costa del Sol.'

'Where did you stay? A hotel?'

'A villa he rented from someone he knew.'

'Any mutual friends who can verify what you have told me?'

'No.'

'Anything else?'

'I've said more than I should have already.'

'You could make a lot of money out of this story.'

'I don't want money. I want him back.'

'Take my card – ring me anytime. I will do some digging around. If I go ahead with the story, I will let you know as soon as.'

Magda pondered whether or not she had done the right thing. She joined Ros later that afternoon.

'I hope I have done the right thing, but he has given me no choice.'

'Magda, listen to me, if things get too tricky for you to handle alone, I might be able to help you.'

'That's very kind, Ros, but I can't see how.'

'I keep telling you that you need a support network, think about it. He has a life and people around him, you live in the shadows and have no one.'

'So, what do I do next? I'm already worried that I have spoken to Rhiannon Roe.'

'I could put you in touch with a contact, who would, for the right price, deal with your problem for you.'

'A contact? What's one of them?'

'A person you could hire to help resolve your problem.'

'Would they go and talk to Rufus, on my behalf?'

'The contact wouldn't go to see Rufus to talk, but would give him a message. Do you understand?'

'Not really.'

'A contact is someone you would hire, who would work on your behalf, do whatever you asked of them.'

'Such as?'

'Hiring a contact allows you to be in control. For example, the subject, Rufus, would be the contact's priority. He would keep you updated on his whereabouts, who he was meeting. He would even use a little muscle if needed.'

'Oh, I don't think there would be any call for that sort of thing.'

'The point is, he would be available to do your bidding.'

'How much would it cost?'

'A lot, but it would be worth it. Put yourself in the driver's seat for once, you call the shots. Think about it.'

CHAPTER NINETEEN

'Mrs Ronson, I should have warned you in advance we were coming home. I will be home for a week or so while Sir Rufus is in London.'

'No problem, madam. It is so good to see you looking so well.'

'Thank you. I will take a shower and get a change of clothes. Then I'll go down to the stables. I can't wait. I have missed everybody and everything here at home so much.'

'I am sure you have. I will put out some clean towels for you, madam.'

'Thank you, Mrs Ronson.'

Daphne was thrilled to be back at Grange Manor. After a shower and a change of clothes she went down to the stables to check on the horses. She had missed them so much. George and the boys had been doing a good job; the horses looked superb. Giving them a hug and a kiss, she could see that they were pleased to see her too.

She made her way back to the house and saw Mrs Ronson waving from the window.

'Lady Holroyd, there is a call for you. A Mr Donald Kemp from the *News of the World*.'

'Wanting to speak to me? Okay, I will take the call in the lounge. Thank you.'

'Lady Holroyd speaking.'

'Donald Kemp here, thank you for taking my call. I'm a reporter with the *News of the World* and I would like to hear your side of the story.'

'What on earth are you talking about?'

'The story released earlier today in the *London Standard*, regarding a romantic liaison between your husband, Sir Rufus, and a much younger woman, Magda Rainford … You haven't read or heard the news today, Lady Holroyd?'

'Is this some kind of hoax?'

'No, Lady Holroyd, I assure you it's not. I would like your comments on the allegations published today.'

'I have nothing to say.'

'I would be happy to come round to get your side of the story. Is your husband available?'

Daphne slammed down the receiver.

The telephone began to ring.

'Mrs Ronson, please unplug the telephone. I don't want to be disturbed.'

Could it be true? Daphne couldn't bear to think of Rufus with another woman. Surely, she would have known if he was seeing someone. She and Rufus had been in Brussels; it was ridiculous. She lived for Rufus. Feeling faint and nauseous, she began to tremble, her body wracked with fear. She ran upstairs, lay on the bed and curled up in a ball, clutching the bedding for dear life. He had always said that she was his first and last love and she had never doubted it.

Rufus was shocked on seeing publication after publication with his photograph on the front page at the news-stands.

He had always worried someone would find out but he had never considered Magda would go to the press. Repeatedly, he tried to ring Daphne, but the line was disconnected. He decided to go home immediately.

It was five o'clock and there was still no sign of Lady Holroyd. Edna James made her way to the kitchen with the farm deliveries and to speak with Mrs Ronson.

Doris Ronson knew there must be something wrong – Edna always came into the kitchen with a flurry of chatter, but today she was quiet and preoccupied.

'What might be troubling you, Edna?'

'I don't know if I should say.'

'Come on now, we have no secrets.'

'Well, this morning I got a call from my sister who lives in Enfield. She told me about a story in the *London Standard* newspaper, about Sir Rufus. Some young lass is claiming she has been having an affair with him.'

'Well, I took a call for Lady Holroyd. It was from a newspaper reporter.'

'What did he want?'

'He wanted to speak to Lady H.'

'About?'

Doris sat at the table. 'I think it was bad news.'

'Why's that, then?'

'Lady Holroyd took the call. I heard her ask if it was a hoax. She came off the phone white as snow and looking completely shell-shocked. Then she took off to her room, not to be disturbed by anyone.'

'You don't think it's true, about His Lordship?'

144

'How should I know? He doesn't tell me what he gets up to. He is away a lot. I suggested she contact him but she said not to trouble him.'

There was a rap on the back door.

'What brings you here at this time, George?'

'Any chance of a cup of tea, Doris? I've got something to show both of you.'

'Let's have a look at it.'

George passed the daily newspaper over to Doris.

'My goodness, I don't believe it. No wonder the poor woman had to go and lie down.'

'Aye, ladies, he's been playing away, with a young 'un too.'

'Sit down, George, I'll get you that tea.'

'There's more inside on page five, Rhiannon Roe's column. He's going to be on all the front pages by this evening.'

'Well, they say there's no smoke without fire.'

'You're right, Doris. Who knows what he gets up to in London.'

'Read it out to us then, George. I don't have my glasses.'

'"Miss Magda Rainford claims that for a number of years she has been the lover of Sir Rufus Holroyd MP, now MEP."'

'Who would have thought. Dirty sod, his poor wife.'

'Hold on a minute, Edna. What if it's all lies?'

'Look, ladies, they wouldn't print it if it wasn't true.'

'I quite agree,' Edna chipped in.

'What if they divorce? What about our jobs?'

'I've been here best part of forty years.'

'So you have, Doris.'

'I am well past retirement age. I love it here.'

Doris didn't like change. She had a routine and a well-organised life at Grange Manor. 'Look out the window. There's reporters everywhere.'

'Should I call the police?'

'No, Doris, they're not doing anything at the moment.'

'They're trespassing.'

'Leave it to the lady of the house to sort out. We're just the hired help.'

'George is right. It's not our place to make them sort of decisions.'

'What's that noise?' George looked through the kitchen window. 'He's back.'

Sir Rufus drove through the gates and sped up to Grange Manor, pursued by the press.

'I'd best go and greet him and pretend I know nothing.' Mrs Ronson almost ran from the kitchen through the corridor to the front door.

'Sir Rufus. You're home early, sir.'

'Mrs Ronson, where is my wife?'

'Upstairs in her room, sir, very upset … er, not feeling too good.'

Rufus ran upstairs and into the bedroom to find Daphne, tense and pale, sitting on the edge of the bed.

Turning towards him with tears rolling down her face, she looked as she did during the decade of darkness when depression and grief had imprisoned her. He couldn't bear to see her in such pain.

'Daphne.'

'Rufus, what's going on?'

'Come downstairs and I will pour us both a brandy.'

'I don't want a brandy. I want to know if it's true.'

He saw the desperation in her eyes.

'Have you been seeing this woman?'

'I don't know what to say.'

'Is it true?'

He knew he was in deep and had to get out of it fast. 'No.'

'Where has this story come from?'

'I don't know. All I know is that it isn't true.'

'Have you ever met this woman?'

He had betrayed his wife and now he was denouncing his love for Magda. 'Once, years ago.'

He had to erase this relationship, sever all connections with Magda and the Chelsea apartment.

The rental agreement wasn't a concern; it was taken out under an alias. The credit card payments and holiday bookings were being dealt with by Cedric. Cedric knew the whole story, and with Cedric's political connections, Rufus hoped his relationship with Magda could disappear into thin air. Cedric had suggested Magda be followed by a private detective and Rufus agreed; any evidence of Magda stepping out of line could be used to label her as a stalker. Rufus knew it was ultimately his responsibility to get rid of Magda, as quietly and calmly as possible. After all, Cedric could only do so much without crossing the line.

Rufus trusted Cedric with his life and it was his life that he was fighting for, his future with Daphne, and his reputation.

The telephone continued to ring constantly. The press wanted some reaction and they had no intention of going away. Rufus and Daphne were advised by their solicitor to meet with the press. The solicitor, Mr Grove, had agreed to read out a statement on their behalf and that they would meet at the gates of Grange Manor the following morning, after which it would hopefully all go away.

Daphne was still stressed but she was now convinced it was all malicious lies.

Rufus and Daphne strolled arm in arm to the gates, while Mr Grove walked ahead of them. The gates opened and the flash bulbs and questions shouted by the press drowned out Mr Grove. The couple stepped forwards and gave the press what they wanted. Against Mr Grove's wishes, Rufus agreed to speak.

'We have been subjected to lies and humiliation by the press, who are so desperate to boost sales they have run a story that cannot be substantiated. I want to clarify here and now that I met Miss Magda Rainford on one occasion, three, possibly four, years ago, when I delivered a speech at a Conservative Party dinner dance. Since then I have never seen nor been in any sort of communication with her. My wife and I ask that we be left in peace to get over this ordeal.'

Rufus kissed his wife and she smiled.

CHAPTER TWENTY

'Hello, Rhiannon Roe speaking.'

'Rhiannon, Mr Scott would like to see you in the office immediately.'

Mr Scott, the proprietor of the newspaper, was in the office today. Rhiannon's body tensed up and her heart was racing.

Why was she worrying? She had done her homework on the story. Maybe he was pleased with the scoop.

Mr Scott was on the telephone when she arrived. Jane, the secretary, ushered her to a seat strategically placed directly opposite the great man himself.

Scott swung around in his chair.

'Right, I want answers. Where did you get your story from?'

'I was approached by Magda Rainford, while at a spa. It was quite by chance.'

'Did you check out your source and her story thoroughly?'

'I did some digging and I believed she was telling me the truth.'

'Why?'

'I just did, call it intuition.'

'Not good enough. Some stranger comes up to you, spins you a yarn, that you don't bother to check out, and then you put it into print.'

'It wasn't quite like that. I ran this by the editor. He gave the green light before it went to print.'

'I'll deal with Jackson. I have spoken briefly with him and I can't believe he approved this crap for publication.'

'Sir, Mr Jackson—'

'Do not start making excuses for him.'

'Mr Scott, I have a gut feeling about this story. I know it's got legs.'

'The only legs I want to see are yours, returning to your desk and drafting an apology. I don't want the paper to be sued over this. Let's deal with it. Write the apology, Rhiannon. Now get out.'

'Sir, we are journalists and it's our duty to dig out the truth and I think Magda Rainford is telling the truth.'

'You have written about a man who is a pillar of our society with no proof.'

'But, sir?'

'Bollocks. With no collaborating evidence we don't have a leg to stand on.'

'What if I get more evidence?'

'You will draft an apology, which Jackson will approve and deal with. Rhiannon, the subject is closed. If you value your position here you will erase this story from your over, fertile mind. If you don't, not only will you be out of a job but they will make sure you never work as a journalist again.'

'Who are they?'

'Get smart. Back to work – we have nothing further to discuss.'

As she reached the door, she looked back at him. As if reading her mind, he pointed his pen at her. 'Forget it.'

Rhiannon sat at her desk. Why was the story being quashed? Why could she not dig further into the matter? It wasn't the first time someone's private life had hit the news without substantiating evidence. The press relies on hearsay. The Holroyds had denied the affair but hadn't provided any means of proving that it wasn't true. Since when did Scott give a damn about protecting pillars of society and what did he mean by 'they'? *They will make sure you never work as a journalist again.* Could it be the security service? The thought unnerved her. She decided she would rather not find out.

'Switchboard, how may I help you?'

'Any calls from Magda Rainford come through for Rhiannon Roe, don't on any account put them through.'

Feeling very uneasy, she thought about Magda Rainford. What was going on in those high places?

CHAPTER TWENTY-ONE

Lakeside spa was Magda's only refuge. Since the story broke, she had been in turmoil. Fortunately, no one knew who she was as only her name had been in print, not her photograph. Rufus had not made contact and she was in limbo about what would happen next. She couldn't go on living at the Chelsea apartment. Or could she? Everything was still being paid for and the credit card hadn't been stopped.

She had gone crazy when Rufus denied knowing her, but now she was getting support from Ros and beginning to feel in control, she wouldn't allow him to erase her from history, their history.

Over lunch, Magda brought Ros up to speed on the situation.

'Ros, I have decided I would like to hire the service of a contact.'

'Be very sure of what you are asking.'

'What do you mean?'

'You must be absolutely certain this is the right thing for you, before going down this road. Be clear in your mind that this is what you want.'

'Are you suggesting I am not of clear mind?'

'No, I don't want you to make a big decision in the heat of the moment.'

'I can afford it.'

'My dear, the cost could be more than financial if this venture is not planned and executed correctly.'

'Rufus needs to be taught a lesson. He can't treat me this way. I'm serious about this.'

'I can see you are. Give me your telephone number and I will arrange the initial introduction. Remember, the contact will be in touch with you. He will give you his terms and conditions. Never instruct him to do anything in the heat of the moment. Once he has your instructions there is no going back, no changing your mind. Be very careful.'

'How long will it take for him to contact me?'

'It will be soon, so make sure you know exactly what you want him to do. After the initial contact he will only contact you when he needs to. You will never be able to contact him. Is that clear?'

'Yes.'

'I will get the ball rolling, but from this moment onwards, you must never speak of this to me again. It will be as if I know nothing.'

'I promise. Thank you for helping me.'

Back in London, things were much the same: noise, traffic, pollution and loneliness. Magda took the Tube into the city centre. She strolled around the big department stores looking at the cosmetic counters. What was the point of it all, make-up, stylish clothes? There was no point without Rufus in her life. She spent the rest of the afternoon at the cinema and then took the Tube back home before rush hour.

She picked up a newspaper and a couple of magazines for the evening ahead. Back at the apartment, she was feeling desolate again.

The phone rang. She was so shaken, she knocked over her glass of wine as she reached for the receiver. Her nerves were in tatters.

'Hello.' She so hoped it was Rufus.

'You have been expecting a call from me, yes?'

For an instant she was confused, then the penny dropped.

'Oh, yes I have. You are the contact.'

'You will know me only as Rhein, yes?' His voice was hard and abrupt.

'Yes.' She couldn't make out the accent, Eastern European maybe.

'Who is the target of my assignment?'

'He is a very prominent man.'

'Just answer the question.'

'Sir Rufus Holroyd MEP, based in Brussels.'

Confusion and doubt started sneaking into her strong resolution.

'What is your first instruction?'

After taking a deep breath and regaining her composure, she said, 'Just observe him. Let me know who he is spending time with, his routine.'

'Just observe, yes?'

'Yes, observation only until further notice.' She tried to sound confident, but she hadn't a clue what she was getting herself into.

'I require payment of £4,000 in cash immediately.'

'Okay. How do I get the money to you?'

'If I am to fly out to Brussels I will need the money tomorrow. This is what you must do. You will go to Westminster Bridge, walk halfway across and then stop. You will be to the left of the bridge, stand, look out at the Thames. I will take the package of money that will be tucked under your left arm and will walk away. Eight o'clock, tomorrow. Future payment will be delivered elsewhere yet to be decided.' The call ended.

She would withdraw the money the following morning and follow his instructions.

Another lonely night ahead, but at least she was doing something at last. She picked up the *London Standard*; while leafing through, she was taken aback to see a photograph of Rufus and Daphne, on page two. Stunned, she read the headline.

'The London Standard wishes to express its sincere apologies to Sir and Lady Rufus Holroyd for a story released a week ago, which stated Sir Rufus was having an affair with a woman named Magda Rainford.' It quoted from the piece Rhiannon Roe had written. *'A woman, Magda Rainford, approached the journalist and alleged she was having an affair with the MEP. The information was unsubstantiated. The London Standard takes full responsibility for the error of judgement in printing this allegation.'*

Magda wondered why Rufus hadn't been in touch – he must be livid – but maybe the press would be watching him closely. Magda only realised the severity of it all when the story made *News at Ten*.

The newscaster began: '*The London Standard* today printed an apology to former MP, now MEP, Sir Rufus Holroyd, and his wife, Daphne, for printing a story claiming Sir Rufus had been having an affair with a woman named Magda Rainford. Sir Rufus strongly denied the affair and claims to have met Miss Rainford on only one occasion.' The programme cut to footage of the Holroyds standing outside their home with the press.

Rufus's tone of voice emphasised his disgust at the allegation. 'This is an unfounded allegation, a slur on my reputation and cause of distress to me and my wife.'

Magda cringed at the thought of her name being bandied about on the news and in newspapers all over the country. Both she and Rufus were in the public eye whether they liked it or not. She poured herself a large whisky to calm her nerves.

What would Daphne think? Had she had her suspicions? Did she believe Rufus? Or were they fronting it out?

The newscaster continued to say that Sir Rufus, having only met Miss Rainford on one occasion, denied their relationship ever existed – that it was pure fantasy. Tears rolled down her cheeks. How could he deny it when she was living here in an apartment that he was renting? The more she drank the more morose she became; the familiar melancholia returned as tears dripped from her eyes.

Sadness was followed by anger churning inside her until it could no longer be contained.

'You bastard.' The glass shattered against the wall.

Shards and fragments of glass scattered across the floor. With bare feet she stamped on the glass, harder and harder. The sharp, sparkling glass pierced her flesh. She was numb to the sensation of the slicing and mutilating of the soles of her feet, until the rage began to wane and was replaced by despair. Her body wracked with pain, the carpet covered with sticky shards, coated in blood, she hobbled to the bathroom, not daring to look at the damage to her feet. A trail of bloody foot marks followed her. She grabbed the shower head and sprayed her feet with water. Her feet stung so badly. She felt faint. Blood continued to rush from gashes, pools of red water filled the shower base. *Oh, what if I bleed to death? Rufus, where are you?*

I need an ambulance.

Propped against the bathroom wall, her feet wrapped in loo roll, she reflected on her situation. Why was she so scared? *We were having an affair; I told the truth.* Why did she fear the press? Her greatest loss was Rufus, and she had been losing him for some time, long before it became public. Rufus was the one with the most to lose, he was the one who told lies. Good old respectable Sir Rufus had been sneaking around with a woman young enough to be his daughter. A woman he denies knowing – what sort of man does this? A man who is scared. Going public had shaken him up. As for his wife, it seems she was going to bury her head in the sand because she wasn't woman enough to stop him straying. What self-respecting woman would allow this? She would not back down. If he wanted a fight then he was going to get one. She had done the right thing hiring Rhein. Rufus needed to be taught a lesson. After all, what could go wrong? As long as she gave clear, precise instructions. She was in control.

The ambulance arrived.

CHAPTER TWENTY-TWO

It was seven fifty. She walked slowly, wincing from the pain of her bandaged feet, along Westminster Bridge in the dark and the rain. She approached the middle of the bridge, package under her left arm, umbrella in her right hand. People scuttled past in an attempt to reach shelter before the heavens opened. She looked out at the dark depths of the Thames; the raindrops made little holes on the surface of the water. Her mind drifted along with the water, on and on the river flowed into oblivion.

Startled as the parcel was pulled from under her arm, she instinctively turned around, face to face with a man with a moustache and brown, dead eyes.

Quickly, she turned back towards the river while he walked away into the crowd and darkness. She shivered.

What had she done? She had seen his face – would he think twice about killing her? How would he do it? He might weigh down her dead body and throw her in the dark, murky Thames. What an eerie end. If she ever saw him again, he might be the last human face she would ever see.

Stationary, on the bridge, frozen, afraid to turn around. Time ticked by.

The panic subsided. She chastised herself. *Snap out of it. I am in control. I give the instructions and pay the money.*

Confidently, she made her way towards the Tube station. She was in charge.

The thought of Rhein flying out to Brussels to monitor Rufus sent a rush of excitement through her body. She was back in the game and making up points, rapidly. How ironic that some of the money Rufus made available to her was now financing surveillance of him.

CHAPTER TWENTY-THREE

A week later, Rhein had little to report. He waited for further instructions. Time was money.

At midnight, the phone rang. 'Magda.'

'Rufus, it's so good to hear your voice. I miss you.'

'Stop it. You stupid bitch, stop this.'

'I can explain.'

'This stops now. I want you out of the apartment. I'll give you a month to get out. By the end of the month the credit card will stop. You should have enough to live on until you find work.'

'But, Rufus, I—'

'Shut up. We never happened. Make a new life for yourself.'

'I don't want to live without you.' She started to plead again.

'If you don't leave me alone, you'll be sorry.'

The line went dead.

She had been sold out, that's it. She was about to lose everything, after three years of having invested in this relationship. He wouldn't change his mind and he wasn't coming back.

With a month to make sure she was secure and to show him she was as strong and empowered as him, she decided it was time to bring him to his knees. She had one last card to play.

Magda was up most of the night working on the plan. At nine thirty in the morning she rang the bank and arranged to withdraw £10,000 from her account. At one o'clock, she collected the money and made her way to Swiss Bank; she sensed she was being followed, so she picked up her pace.

'I am here to see the manager. I did ring earlier.'

'Please take a seat.'

The bank manager appeared within seconds. 'Good day.'

'Hello, I need to use a safe deposit box.'

'Ah, yes. Please follow me.'

She was allocated safe deposit box number 105. She took the £10,000 from her bag and placed it in the box and locked it.

'I will need to leave the key with the bank. These are my instructions, a man named Mr Rh … Mr Razz will arrive at the bank in the next couple of days. He will ask for this key, which must be given to him. He should not be asked for identification. Just give the key to him. The contents of the box will be taken by him.'

'This is highly irregular, but if you insist. I will need you to sign a document stating these are your instructions.'

'Of course. Could you do this now? I will wait in reception.'

'Yes.'

Magda waited only a short time before the manager returned.

'Just sign at the bottom of the page.'

Without reading the document, she signed.

'Thank you, Mr Charles.'

'Thank you, Miss Rainford.'

Rhein rang.

'I will soon run out of money. I will pay you £10,000, for this final instruction. I want you to do something to Rufus Holroyd, to shake him up in some way.'

'What exactly must I do?'

'You're the expert.'

'Break a leg, shoot him in the shoulder?'

'No. Too drastic. Don't hurt him badly. I want him to feel pain, I want a mark left on his body to remember me by.'

She gulped the whisky.

'Where do I collect the money?'

'I have placed the money in a safe deposit box at Swiss Bank, central London. Ask to see the manager, tell him your name is Mr Razz. He will give you key 105. No identification will be required. Take the money and then it's goodbye.'

He hung up.

Magda knew there was no going back.

Magda grabbed her coat and suitcase, and left for Lakeside Spa. She needed to get away from the apartment and be among people, experience some normality. She was tired of being a little dormouse.

While away, she would consider a further plan of action. Until she knew what Rufus's reaction was to be following his visit from Rhein, she was unable to plan with certainty. She would return to London in two days, to see how the land lay.

Magda was on a high throughout her train journey. She smiled to herself; she was proud of the proactive plans she had put into place.

Once in her room, she rang reception and booked numerous treatments, ordered room service and took advantage of every little luxury available to her. This way of life was about to end. 'Let's max out the credit card while we can.'

Back in Brussels, Rhein made a call.

'She gave the instruction.'

'You know what you must do.'

He returned to his hideout and locked the door behind him. He took a slim black case from the wardrobe and lifted out a Browning 9mm semi-automatic gun. He loaded a magazine with bullets and attached it to his holster strapped across his shoulder along with the gun, ready for the next day. Another gloomy evening. He couldn't go out. No one could recognise him should anything go wrong. Once the job was done, he was out of there.

Refreshed, Magda made the journey back to Chelsea, arriving home in the early evening. Through the communal entrance and up the stairs to her apartment. She was about to put the key in the door when she realised it was slightly ajar. She pushed the door open and cautiously stepped inside. It had been forced almost off its hinges; the lock was broken. Every door to every room had been flung open. She glanced from room to room; it was obvious the place had been turned over, ransacked. Her immediate thought was to let Rufus know, then she realised that was no longer an option. Should she call the police? Furniture and personal effects had been thrown, drawers ripped out, clothing strewn across the floor. *Bloody thieves.*

She went into the bedroom to check the damage. A photograph of Rufus she kept by her bedside had gone. She searched among the debris; it wasn't there. She went into the bathroom and saw that his robe and toiletries had gone. Had Rufus been here? Someone had – they had cleared the place of anything belonging to Rufus. This was a deliberate break-in, to erase him from her life.

All the tranquillity she had experienced on leaving the spa had diminished. The adrenaline flowed through her veins. Back to living on her nerves.

Rufus had said she had a month to get out of the apartment; clearly, he wanted her out now.

Magda didn't go to bed in case the intruders returned; although they had taken what they came for, she couldn't be sure they wouldn't come back. She remained fully clothed should she need to make a run for it. The front door was jammed closed with the heavy dining room table. She decided to stay sober and remain alert. The television and radio would remain off. A small lamp was all she needed and she would listen carefully for any sounds outside the apartment.

In the early hours she fell asleep.

After waking up at mid-day, she splashed her face with cold water and then nipped out to check the newspapers. She flicked through each one briefly; there was no further mention of their affair. She bought a coffee and a pastry and took them home, settling down in front of the television for the lunchtime news. It was announced that a terrorist attack had taken place in Brussels.

164

'A failed attack on the lives of members of the European Parliament has taken place, outside the European Union headquarters in Brussels. One of the terrorists was shot dead at the scene. It has not yet been determined which terrorist organisation was responsible for the attack.'

Magda knew it would be difficult for Rhein to carry out his final instruction as Brussels would be buzzing with security. He might call her this evening for further instructions as the current circumstances would make his job impossible.

When he hadn't called by 1 a.m., she wondered if Rhein had taken the money from Swiss Bank. If he couldn't fulfil the arrangement, he shouldn't get the money.

The next day she hurried to Swiss Bank.

'Is it possible to see the manager? It is very important.'

'Do you have an appointment?'

'No, but it's urgent.'

'Do you have an account with us?'

'No. If I could explain, a few days ago I used your safe deposit box facility. I need to speak to the manager about this.'

'The manager has been at head office for a few days; he only returned this morning. I will ask if he is available. Please take a seat.'

Thirty minutes she waited, and still no sign of the manager. Magda returned to the counter.

'Miss Rainford, sorry I left you waiting. He will be with you as soon as he is able. You can imagine he has returned to the branch with a lot of work. If you wouldn't mind waiting a bit longer.'

Magda returned to her seat, irritated and tense.

A short time later a middle-aged man walked towards her and held out his hand.

'Miss Rainford, how may I help you?'

'Are you a new manager? I met with Mr Charles a few days ago.'

'I am Mr Charles, and have always been the manager here. Perhaps you met with one of my colleagues.'

'I want to know if Mr Razz collected the money that I left for him in the safe deposit box?'

'I am sorry, Miss Rainford, but I don't know to what you are referring. I have no knowledge of the arrangement. Mr Razz, you say?'

She nodded.

'Please bear with me. One of my staff must have seen you. If you would kindly take a seat I will go and check the system and with staff who were on duty.'

He was gone for some time. All she wanted to know was if the money had been collected.

He returned, shaking his head. 'I have checked the records, spoken to staff and there is no paperwork showing any money being put into our vault.'

'Are you sure? I did sign a piece of paper.'

'Do you have a copy?'

'No.'

'The bank representative would always give the customer a copy of any transaction or agreement.'

She stared at him in disbelief. 'I was here a few days ago. I signed an agreement regarding the £10,000, which was put in a safety deposit box, number 105.'

She could tell Mr Charles had no idea what she was talking about.

Something told her to get the hell out of there.

'Miss Rainford, are you sure it was this bank?'

Magda broke out in a cold sweat. 'Yes, I know which bank I was at.'

'I have checked the system and spoken with staff who were on duty. No one knows anything about it.'

'What's happening?' she heard herself say.

'Shall I call the police?'

Magda panicked. She left the bank and headed down the high street. The news-stands had up-to-date copies of the dailies and on the front of all of them was a photograph of Rhein. Magda bought a newspaper and fled back to the apartment. What was happening? Why was Rhein being labelled a terrorist? Was he a terrorist? Or a terrorist and a contact? Who the hell was he?

Was her life under threat? Magda looked up a much-needed telephone number.

CHAPTER TWENTY-FOUR

'Sir Rufus, I have the police on the telephone.'

'Put them through.'

'Good afternoon, sir. Just to let you know that your home and office have additional security, including undercover police surveillance.'

'That is very reassuring, Inspector. Has anything else materialised?'

'No, sir. I think it best if you were to remain at home for a week or so.'

'No.' Rufus had no intention of hiding away.

'We don't want another attempt on your life.'

'If the police do their job properly, I should have nothing to worry about.'

'Are you quite sure you have no idea of anyone who could be behind this attack, a personal grudge?'

'How many times do I have to say this? No,' Rufus answered defensively.

'Sir, any information, no matter how trivial, could help us. Your wife could be targeted next.'

'You don't think …? I mean, you did say it was a terrorist operation,' he spluttered.

'That is all we can report to the public at present. We will keep your name out of the public domain for the time being. We are working closely with Scotland Yard and MI6 will have been briefed. We all need to work together.'

'What about the other European MEPs and the British MEPs?'

'They, too, are to receive protection and guidance. We don't know if the attack was random or if it was personal.'

Magda dialled an office number.

'Hello.'

'Hello, Emma. It's Magda.'

'Magda Rainford? Good gracious, where have you been hiding yourself? It's been years.'

'Yes, I know, forgive me. Look, I need your help. I need to see you as soon as possible.'

'Is this linked to Rufus Holroyd? I do read the papers. What on earth is going on?'

'I know we haven't seen each other in ages and I can't explain over the phone.'

'If it's urgent, I could meet you at lunchtime.'

'Tomorrow lunchtime, could we meet tomorrow? It's so important.'

'Er, yes, where?'

'At the Veggie's restaurant on Chelsea high street, one o'clock.'

'Okay. Make it one fifteen, to give me time to get across town. Magda, is there something terribly wrong?'

'I'll explain tomorrow. Emma, just jot down my telephone number.'

'I've got that. So, you're still in London?'

'Yes. I will explain everything tomorrow.'

Magda arrived at Veggie's on time and ordered a mineral water. The waiter hovered until she told him she would wait for a friend to join her before she ordered. By three o'clock, it was still a no-show from Emma. Magda tried to call Emma's office number from the restaurant payphone, but the line was permanently engaged. Perhaps she couldn't make it. She might have been delayed or had an accident. Magda returned to the table.

'I am sorry, my friend hasn't turned up.'

She had been sitting there for two hours. She put on her coat and picked up her bag, but then she began to panic again. She needed to get home. She pushed open the restaurant's heavy glass door. The noise of the traffic attacked her senses, causing her to jump. She rushed along the high street, trying to avoid all the people who got in her way, yet still they bumped into her. Everyone seemed to be deliberately stopping her from getting where she wanted to be. Her shoulder bag was knocked from her arm and the contents fell to the ground; she bent down to pick them up.

'Bastard,' she muttered. A man in a grey suit and raincoat caught her eye. He looked away. Magda's unease intensified. After gathering all her belongings together, she continued to walk at a pace. She turned to see he was still behind her. Her heart thudded; she began to run. The man speeded up too. He was weaving between the people out shopping. She dashed down the steps into the Tube station. She had her ticket already; she hurried through the barriers and down the escalator. A train was in, so she pushed her way through the crowded platform and jumped onto the train just before the doors closed. She took a deep breath as the train moved out of the station her eyes fixed on the platform. That man didn't appear. She had got away.

Sweating heavily, she tried to slow down her breathing. Gradually, she began to calm down. Two stops along she disembarked, crossed the platform and took a Tube back home.

Was that man following me? Or was he just a weirdo? Did I overreact?

At the apartment she took off all her clothes; they were soaked in sweat. Hot and sticky, she showered while reliving the afternoon. Had she seen the man before?

Yes, she had seen him looking through the window of the restaurant. Had he been waiting around? Had she seen his reflection in the shop windows? She knew she hadn't imagined it, but perhaps she had panicked unnecessarily.

At eight o'clock the phone rang. The call was from a payphone.

'Magda.'

'Emma, where were you?'

'Listen, I don't have time to explain. I think you need to be careful. I don't know what's going on or what you have got yourself involved in, but it's best you don't call me again. I think both the home telephone and my work number are being bugged. Sorry, I can't help, please forgive me and take care.' The line went dead.

Magda tried to return the call, but to no avail.

The following day, in desperation, Magda rang the Standard newspaper office, but Rhiannon Roe was not available to take her call, so she left a message.

What to do next? I need to speak to Ros.

She rang Lakeside Spa.

'Hello, Magda Rainford speaking. I wonder if you could help me. During my stays at the spa, I have become friendly with a lady, Mrs Rosalind Bartholomew. I really need to contact her – could you possibly give me her telephone number?'

'I'm afraid not. Clients' personal details are confidential.'

'Could you tell me if she is with you at the moment or due to stay with you soon?'

'Again, I am very sorry, madam. I could take a message and pass it on to the lady. However, we cannot be held responsible if she doesn't receive it.'

'I will leave a message. Please give her my name and contact details and ask if she will contact me as soon as she can.'

'We will endeavour to do so, madam.'

It had been Ros who said she should teach Rufus a lesson, show him she wasn't some bimbo. She felt worse than a bimbo.

Who was Ros Bartholomew?

There was an almighty crash as the door to her apartment was completely knocked off its hinges. Armed police stormed in.

'Stay right where you are. Magda Rainford, I am arresting you on suspicion of a terrorist offence. You do not need to say anything but anything you do say will be taken down and may be used as evidence against you in a court of law. Do you understand?'

'Yes?'

A terrified Magda was bundled into a black van and driven away.

She was taken to the local police station where she was cautioned on a charge of incitement to murder. While in a cell she could hear the hustle and bustle at the station and could sense the gravity of her situation. What should she do? She was helpless, confused and scared.

A police officer entered the cell and brought her a cup of tea.

'What's happening? How long am I to be kept here?' she asked.

'Sorry, madam.' The officer shrugged his shoulders.

Another half hour passed by. The cell, door opened and she was led through the station to an interview room. She sat at the table and was told a duty solicitor would be present shortly. Opposite her sat two police officers, a man and a woman.

'I am Chief Inspector Davidson of the anti-terrorist team and this is Sergeant Benson.'

She couldn't believe it, the anti-terrorist team? She observed them closely. DCI Davidson was about forty-five years old, an unpleasant-looking man who was overweight and sounded out of breath when he spoke. He had an unhealthy pallor, hard deep-set eyes and an abrupt manner. The sergeant appeared equally hardnosed. She was in her mid to late thirties, a tall woman with short black hair, spectacles and no make-up.

'Hello. I am Mr Kay, duty solicitor.'

The police officers left the room while Mr Kay had a private consultation with his client. He smiled weakly at Magda and shook her hand. He was the first person in the last few hours to make her feel human. Twenty minutes later, disclosure completed, the police officers returned to conduct the interview.

Davidson put the cassette tape in the recording machine and commenced the interview.

'This interview is taking place at Chelsea police station on the 21st of September 1993 at 21.09. The interview will be conducted by myself, DCI Davidson of the anti-terrorist team, and Sergeant Benson. Also present is the duty solicitor on behalf of Miss Magda Rainford.'

Davidson looked at Magda.

'You are Miss Magda Rainford? Address: Apartment 10, Kings Court Apartments, Kings Way, in the Borough of Kensington and Chelsea.'

'Yes.'

'Date of birth 12.6.70?'

'Yes.'

'You have been arrested on suspicion of incitement to murder members of the European Parliament. The assassination attempt was carried out in Brussels on the 18th of September 1993 by an as yet unidentified accomplice of Eastern European origin.'

As Davidson continued, Magda drifted into her own world. Her mouth was very dry, her eyes itched and her body ached.

The interrogation went on for what seemed like ages. Davidson became more abrasive as time ticked by; he repeated the same questions over and over again, even the ones that she had answered. Her answers differed each time he asked the same question. She was exhausted and irritated. Would it ever end?

'I had an affair with Sir Rufus Holroyd, for three years, as stated in the press.'

Davidson looked at Benson, and sighed and said in a tone of resignation, 'So, you had an affair with Sir Rufus Holroyd?'

'Yes.'

Davidson glanced at everyone around the table, frustration etched across his bloated face. Narrowing his eyes, he asked Magda, 'Didn't Sir Rufus Holroyd deny this claim on national television?'

Magda squirmed and shuffled her feet. 'Yes, he did, he was lying,' she replied angrily.

'He was lying? Or are you lying?'

'I am telling the truth!'

'There is more to this than you are saying. Come on, let's have it,' Benson urged.

'Okay, I'll tell you everything. I have nothing to hide.'

'Go ahead.' Davidson sat back.

'I was having an affair with Rufus for three years.'

Davidson and Benson stared blankly at her.

'The relationship was floundering, he wanted to get rid of me.'

'Get rid of you?' Benson pressed.

'End the relationship, that's what I mean. So, I spoke to Rhiannon Roe, journalist at the *London Standard*. That's how they came to print that stuff about us.' She shivered.

'Is that it?' Davidson snapped.

There was a pause and Magda nodded.

'What else have you to say? We are listening to you, Magda,' he coaxed.

Magda mumbled, 'I hired a contact.'

'A contact, what's one of those?'

'A sort of hardman, although I really didn't realise that was what he was at first.'

The officers leaned forwards, towards her.

'You're saying you hired a hardman?' Davidson repeated in disbelief.

'Yes, to keep an eye on Rufus. I was losing him, you see. When Rufus told me it was all over between us, I wanted to teach him a lesson.'

'Go on.'

'I instructed Rhein.'

'Hold on, who is Rhein?'

'Rhein was the contact, the hardman.'

'He told you his name, this hardman?'

'Yes, but I don't think it was his real name. Anyway, I just instructed him to hurt Rufus, rough him up a bit, not to kill him or anything so bad.'

'Just rough him up?' he repeated.

'And did he rough him up?' Benson asked.

'I don't know, but he got the blame for the attempted murder of MEPs.'

'How do you know he got the blame?'

'I saw his photograph on the front pages of the newspapers.'

'Oh, so you knew what your hardman looked like – you had met him?'

'I met him only once.'

'Do you expect us to believe that a hired thug would introduce himself to the person who hired him? Give his name and show his face? Come on, what do you take us for?' Davidson thumped the table.

'I really don't think your aggressive tone is helping the situation,' Mr Kay said.

'It's the truth.' Tears ran down Magda's face.

'This is the truth?' Davidson spat, his face red. 'This is an investigation of incitement to murder. Also, this is my investigation – do not tell me how to run it,' he bellowed at Mr Kay.

Davidson told Benson to get four coffees.

'For the tape, Sergeant Benson is leaving the room at 22.13 hours.'

Tapping his pen on the table, Davidson turned back to Magda. 'Don't make things more difficult for yourself than they already are. Just cooperate with us; don't put yourself on the line for those bastards.'

'What bastards?'

Davidson slammed his pen on the table and folded his arms as he turned away.

Benson returned with the coffees. Wearily, Davidson switched the tape back on.

'Sergeant Benson has returned to the room at 22.18 hours. Let me summarise what you have told us so far. You had a three-year relationship with Sir Rufus Holroyd. Sir Rufus wanted to end the relationship but you didn't, and therefore, you hired a hardman to rough up Sir Rufus.'

'Yes.'

'I have two questions, Miss Rainford. Firstly, what did you hope to achieve by having Sir Rufus hurt?'

'I wanted to get back at him. I didn't want him to ignore me.'

'But surely he would never have thought that you were behind the attack on his person. Did you intend to let him know after he had been hurt that you had arranged this attack?'

'I don't know. I hadn't thought that far ahead.'

'You hadn't thought that far ahead?' Davidson paused. 'It sounds pretty pointless to me. You hire a hardman to cause injury to the man you love. One wrong move and Sir Rufus could have been killed. Did you not worry that this might happen?'

Magda rubbed her eyes, desperately trying to stay awake.

'So, Sir Rufus had no idea that he was under threat from you. Is that correct?'

'Yes.'

'What on earth did you hope to achieve?'

'I don't know. I mean, I just wanted … I couldn't allow him to simply walk away. I had no other option.'

Davidson scratched his forehead. 'My second question is in two parts. How did you initially contact a hardman and where did you get the money to pay for his services?'

'I used money left to me in a trust fund.'

'Do you have receipts or bank statements?'

'There will be records at the bank. I have statements for the withdrawal of the money.'

'What do you live on? You don't work.'

'I have been using a credit card given to me by Rufus. He deals with the rent and bills.'

'Do you have credit card statements to support your story of a relationship with Sir Rufus?'

'No. I had the credit card. The bills and statements were dealt with by Rufus.'

'The officers who are searching your apartment will find any financial statements along with other personal effects pertaining to Sir Rufus?'

'I doubt they will find much. My apartment was turned over a few days ago.'

'Did you report this?'

'No.'

'Well, that's convenient,' he snapped.

'Why not investigate the rental agreement, for the Chelsea apartment? It sure isn't in my name.'

'We will. The second part of my question, if you would kindly answer, is how did you find the hardman?'

'Through a woman I became friendly with. She told me about this service and sort of arranged it for me.'

'Who is the woman?'

'I don't know her name.'

'Rubbish! Who is she?'

'I told you I don't know.'

'Let me tell you, young lady, I don't think this woman exists. Where did you meet her?'

'It doesn't matter.'

'It matters all right. Now, where did you meet her?'

Magda jumped. Her mind was a jumbled mess. She had promised not to involve Rosalind. She wouldn't tell them; she would keep her promise.

'I would rather not say.'

'Do you realise the gravity of your situation? Let me tell you, Miss Rainford, if your account of the circumstances and your evidence doesn't improve and you continue to fail to cooperate, you may find yourself going away for a very long time.'

Magda took a deep breath. 'Everything I have told you is the truth.'

'Then tell us the name of the woman?'

'I don't know her name.'

'Then tell us where you met her. Did you meet her once, twice?'

'A few times, that's all I am going to say.'

'Okay. We're not going to get any further tonight. I will just run through what you have told us so far. You admit you had contact with the man shot dead in Brussels, who has been reported as being a terrorist and who you say told you his name was Rhein. Correct?'

'Yes.'

'But you deny having any affiliation to a terrorist organisation?'

'That's right.'

'Even though the security forces believe that the man killed was a terrorist?'

'Yes.'

'You said you were put in touch with the man you refer to as Rhein, by a woman you met only a few times, you refuse to give the woman's name and refuse to say where you met her. Could this woman be a terrorist?'

'No, she isn't a terrorist.'

'But that is what you said about the man killed by security in Brussels. You have no witnesses, no one to confirm anything that you have told us. I am going to end this interview. This is your last opportunity for now to tell us what we need to know.'

Magda's head was bowed; she didn't move.

Davidson took a deep breath. 'This interview has ended at 23.00.'

Magda was returned to the cell for the night.

The next morning, she was escorted in a police van to appear in court. The evidence given by the prosecution to the magistrate stated that her interview with the police was a cover story, to protect members of a terrorist organisation. The magistrate agreed that she should be remanded in custody and she was charged with incitement to murder. The defence barrister requested bail, but was refused.

The numbness turned to hysteria. She had told them the truth – how could she be a terrorist? The decision had been made. She was powerless. The police doctor urged her to take a tranquiliser and recommended they be given three times a day to keep her calm.

Magda spent the next two and a half months on remand in Holloway prison awaiting trial at the Crown Court.

Magda's solicitor for the trial was a Mr Lacy. Mr Lacy had visited Magda while she was on remand in Holloway prison, and these regular visits assisted him in working on her defence. He had recommended she be represented by a barrister who he had worked with on numerous occasions, a Mr Bowles QC, a barrister who thrived on a challenge, and challenging it would be with the lack of information Mr Lacy had gathered from Magda. Due to the magnitude of the evidence against her, Mr Lacy had recommended she plead guilty.

'I am not pleading guilty, I am innocent.'

'Your account is full of flaws. There are no witnesses. I implore you to name the woman who put you in contact with the hardman.'

'I can't do that.'

'Miss Rainford, we have no one to corroborate your story. Sir Rufus has made a statement that he only met you on one occasion. Is there anyone who saw you out together, any friends you told of your relationship?'

'No.'

'This will go to trial with no concrete evidence, just your account.'

'I told you about Emma Fairchild and her family. I was with them the evening I met Rufus.'

'They told me this but have no knowledge of you having an affair with Sir Rufus. They said you simply dropped off the radar.'

'I had to, to protect Rufus.'

Mr Lacy found Magda's story to be full of gaps and hearsay. There were no witnesses to anything she had told him.

'Miss Rainford, I am pleading with you to name the woman who gave you the details of the contact.'

CHAPTER TWENTY-FIVE

The trial date was to be set for the new year. Mr Bowles QC visited Magda, along with Mr Lacy, on a number of occasions to give her his advice and to take her instructions.

'I have deep concern for the outcome of this trial. We have no witnesses to support anything you have told us. Your account of the events of the past three years is shaky to say the least. I implore you to tell us the name of the woman you claim to have met. Without this woman we have nothing. It's your only chance.'

Magda knew he was right but she had promised not to involve Ros.

Again, she refused.

A few of Magda's neighbours confirmed she resided at the Chelsea apartment but could not confirm Sir Rufus's visits. No one paid any attention to visitors. Most people were out at work and led busy lives.

The women on the wing were fascinated by Magda and the charges against her. Most of them were inside for shop-lifting, violence, drugs and petty crime. Magda's impending trial was in the papers; she had been charged with incite-ment to murder – that was big.

Magda shared a cell with Cindy Knowles. Cindy had been charged with drug offences and was familiar with the four walls of a cell.

'Hey, Magda, are you sure you don't want a roll up?' Cindy swung her legs around, as she perched on the upper bunk.

'No, I have never smoked and am not starting now.'

'Tell me that when you get a long stretch. You'll be gagging for a fag to kill the boredom. Why did you admit to knowing the … what do they call him? … a contact, the hardman?'

'I was telling the truth. I did hire him, but I didn't want him to kill Rufus, just rough him up. He was no terrorist. That's the bit I don't get myself. I was told he was a contact, like a private detective who would go that bit further.'

'What was he like, this fella of yours?'

'He was everything to me. My future and my life, I had nothing to live for without him.'

'So that's why you got heavy? I mean, having him hurt wasn't going to send him running back to you, was it?'

'I guess not, but I knew I had lost him.'

'What was it like living in an upmarket pad in Chelsea?'

'It was fabulous for a while, but it became lonely. We had to keep a low profile just in case anyone recognised him.'

'I'm surprised he wasn't recognised being an MP and then a Euro MP.'

'He didn't have a high public profile, unlike now.'

'Well, at least you can say you lived a bit, girl.'

'But I am innocent.'

'That's what all first-timers say.'

'But I am.'

'Don't go down that road, Mags. Everyone will get brassed off with you. We're all innocent in here, you know.'

Magda lay on the bottom bunk and closed her eyes. What the hell was going on?

You get slated for telling the truth by both the law and the inmates.

CHAPTER TWENTY-SIX

On the morning of the trial, Magda was taken from Holloway in a prison van to the Old Bailey. There were flashing bulbs from press photographers as she was driven into the tunnel under the court building.

From the court cells, Magda was led into the dock handcuffed to a prison officer.

The public gallery was packed, and journalists crammed into the court, eager for scandal. Plain-clothed policemen had been strategically placed around the court room. Chatter and shuffling came from the public gallery, the greatest show on earth was about to begin, the atmosphere was electric.

'Silence in Court. All rise.'

Mr Justice Jacobs entered the courtroom in his wig and scarlet gown. He bowed and the legal teams bowed back. He seated himself on the bench, his expression stern.

'Be seated.'

Magda glanced at the barristers in their black gowns and wigs. The jury was sworn in and the barrister for the prosecution, Mr Anthony Pope QC, rose to his feet and began to address them.

'Ladies and gentlemen, you see before you a woman charged with incitement to murder. The defendant, Miss Magda Rainford, was arrested on the 21st of September 1993. The actual murder attempt was carried out on the 19th of September in central Brussels. It was an attack on the lives of members of the European Parliament. It is only thanks to the security services and the British police force that the terrorist did not succeed in his or their bid at a random assassination. The police must be commended at their swift action on the arrest of the defendant. Fortunately, no one targeted was hurt. The plan backfired, resulting in the death of one of the terrorists.' Mr Pope QC turned and pointed towards Magda. He raised his voice.

'You see before you a terrorist, a woman who refuses to name the organisation to which she belongs. Remember, ladies and gentlemen of the jury, had this vicious attack not been thwarted the result could have been devastation, not only for the MEPs in Brussels, but carnage on the streets of Brussels for innocent people. Innocent people like yourselves.' Mr Pope QC turned to address the entire courtroom.

'Magda Rainford is a dangerous woman and she is a manipulator of the truth.'

He looked towards the jury. He lowered his voice and spoke slowly.

'You are entitled to the whole truth and I intend to reveal that truth to you. I am confident you will ensure justice is carried out.'

The entire jury and courtroom looked towards Magda. She felt as if the jury had already decided on their verdict.

The prosecution case began with evidence of the shooting incident. An in-depth account was given by a forensic expert, the jury being referred to their bundle of diagrams and photographs taken at the scene of the shooting. They made notes on the intricacies of the information. This took most of the morning and because of the level of concentration required by the jury, the judge allowed a short interval for refreshments before returning to the trial.

'My lord, I call our next witness.'

'Call Chief Inspector Davidson.'

Davidson walked purposefully towards the witness box and took the oath to tell the truth.

'Chief Inspector Davidson, is it correct during the interviews with the defendant you gave Magda Rainford the opportunity to provide you with the name of the woman who arranged contact between Miss Rainford and the terrorist or, as the defendant refers to him, the "hardman"?'

'Yes, sir.'

'What was her attitude to your questions?'

'She refused to cooperate, sir.'

Mr Justice Jacobs was seen to make a note of this answer and the jury stared hard at the woman in the dock.

The prosecution's case was having an impact on the jury. They were focused on the defendant's lack of cooperation and the withholding of information. The prosecution relied heavily on the evidence of the police. The evidence given by both Davidson and his sergeant was Pope's main focus.

Mr Bowles QC, on behalf of the defendant, began his questioning.

'Inspector Davidson, during the interview with the defendant did she give her account of what led to the shooting in Brussels?'

'Yes, she told us of her alleged affair with Sir Rufus Holroyd. Which has no bearing on the terrorist attack.'

'Didn't she tell you that she knew the man who was shot dead in Brussels?'

'Yes, she said his name was Rhein, and that she had hired him to rough up Sir Rufus.'

'Wouldn't you say that she did cooperate with the police but that her account didn't quite fit with what you wanted to hear?'

'Sir, with all due respect, Miss Rainford was charged with incitement to murder. Not roughing up Sir Rufus.'

'My point, Inspector, is that Miss Rainford did cooperate. She did answer your questions. She told the truth as she saw it.'

'Put like that, I suppose she did.'

'No more questions, my lord.'

Sergeant Benson took the oath. Mr Pope QC stood up.

'Sergeant Benson, Miss Rainford lived in an exclusive apartment block in Chelsea. How did she pay for this luxury?'

'There was no signed rental agreement, an arrangement was made between the letting agents and a man named Mr S Smith.'

Magda could not believe what she was hearing.

'The letting agency said Mr Smith made a cash payment up front, at the beginning of each financial year, every April.'

'Have you been able to locate Mr Smith?'

'No. The letting agency never met him in person. It was arranged over the telephone. As such large payments were made in advance, they didn't feel the need to deal with him on a face-to-face basis.'

'This is an unusual way to run a business.'

'Yes, it is unorthodox, but the agency decided it was safe to enter into this arrangement as there was no concern over payment. All utility bills were paid by the agency on behalf of Mr Smith, a private agreement made between them.'

'What about the credit card bills, where did they go?'

'They went to an empty office, in Bethnal Green. It was rented out at what is referred to as a peppercorn rent. The office is in a neglected area, almost derelict.'

'Who paid these bills?'

'Again, Mr Smith.'

'Do you have any records or information on file regarding Mr Smith?'

'No, sir. He may not be a British citizen – he deals in cash and could be anywhere in the world.'

'So, we have a Mr Smith, responsible for the rental of the Chelsea apartment. What did Miss Rainford tell you when you interviewed her regarding this new information?'

'Miss Rainford said she did not know a Mr Smith, and again insisted Sir Rufus Holroyd was the person renting the apartment.'

'She stuck to her story?'

'Yes, sir.'

'Who is she protecting, by continuing with this charade? No more questions, my lord. Thank you, Sergeant Benson.'

Mr Bowles QC stood. 'Sergeant Benson, this information came to light after the defendant had been charged with incitement to murder.'

'Yes, sir, the investigation was ongoing. Exceptionally, we were allowed to question the defendant because the findings were so pertinent to the case.'

'Miss Rainford made a statement to the police that she does not know a Mr Smith.'

'Yes, sir. As I said to Mr Pope, she insisted Sir Rufus Holroyd rented the apartment.'

'Well, someone certainly did.'

'We have found no evidence linking Sir Rufus to the apartment rental.'

'Without Mr Smith, we are left in limbo, are we not?'

'Yes, sir.'

'But Miss Rainford's relationship with the person who was paying the apartment rent is not the sole purpose of the investigation. This trial is not about an illicit or a non-illicit relationship. It is about incitement to murder. No more questions, my lord.'

At the end of a long day, Mr Bowles QC and his junior barrister, Miss Frost, visited Magda in the court cells.

'Miss Rainford, I may have no other choice but to put you in the witness box, to give your side of the story. Without the name of the woman who put you in touch with the contact, we have little evidence in support of your account.'

'Things aren't looking good?'

'No, not good at all. Miss Rainford, you know what you must do. It is your decision.'

The court was again packed with journalists, reporters and members of the public fortunate enough to have got a seat in the public gallery.

Mr Bowles QC made an opening speech to the court.

'It is my intention to allow Miss Magda Rainford to give the court her own account of what led to her arrest on the 21st of September 1993.'

Magda took the oath and stood silently in the witness box. A sea of faces swam before her eyes.

Mr Bowles QC said, 'Miss Rainford, please tell the court of your involvement in the recent terrorist attack.'

'I am not a terrorist. I don't know any terrorists.'

'But you knew the man who was shot dead as a terrorist?'

Magda spoke quietly. 'The man to whom the press and police refer as a terrorist, the man killed in Brussels by the security services, wasn't a terrorist. He was a contact or hardman I had hired.'

'Miss Rainford, why would you hire a hardman?'

'I didn't hire him to kill anyone. Just to observe at first.'

'Observe whom or what?'

'Sir Rufus Holroyd.'

There was a gasp throughout the courtroom.

'Please tell the court why?'

'I wanted Rufus, er, Sir Rufus, followed. We had been seeing each other for three years.'

'Seeing each other? Please, clarify this statement for the court.'

'We had been having an affair.'

More chatter rang out from the public gallery; the press were scribbling fiercely.

'Silence,' called out Mr Justice Jacobs.

'Miss Rainford, explain to the jury the reason why, if, as you allege, you were having an affair with Sir Rufus, you would want to have him followed and why you would hire such a person as a "hardman" to do so.'

'I wanted him followed because he had moved to Brussels and had taken his wife with him. I felt he was trying to get rid of me, dump me.'

'Why not engage the services of a private detective? Why hire a person of dubious character?'

'Because I thought I would have more power if I put a professional on the job.'

She paused.

'I had become quite depressed. I was desperate. I didn't want to lose him. I instructed Rhein – that was his name – I instructed him to rough up Rufus. I know it sounds crazy but that's what I did.'

'Then what happened?'

'The next thing I knew, Rhein's photograph was on the front page of every newspaper, branded a terrorist.'

'Are you saying that not only were you having an affair with a prominent member of parliament for three years, but also that you hired someone to observe and then cause injury to the man you profess to love?'

'Like I said, I wasn't thinking straight.'

'Where on earth did you find this man?'

'A woman I met at Lakeside Spa arranged it for me.'

'A woman. What woman?'

Magda began to feel faint.

'You are on oath. Could we have a glass of water for Miss Rainford? Miss Rainford, the name of the woman.'

'Rosalind Bartholomew.'

Journalists were up on their feet amid the rising noise from the public gallery.

'Silence in court. We shall reconvene after lunch at 2.15 p.m.'

Mr Justice Jacobs rose.

'All rise.'

Magda returned to the witness box.

'Miss Rainford, you earlier told the court the man you hired was named Rhein. How did you know his name?'

'He told me his name.'

'He told you his name?'

'Yes. I recognised his face on the photograph in the newspapers, because I had seen him before.'

'When did you see him?'

'I delivered a cash payment to him.'

'Where did this transaction take place?'

'On Westminster Bridge.'

'The man allowed you to see him, when he came to Westminster Bridge to collect money from you?'

'Yes. I know it sounds unlikely but that's what happened. I wasn't supposed to turn around. It was instinct. I turned to face him as he took the package with the money from under my arm.'

'Moving on, in your statement to the police you said, "Rhein rang me for further instructions".'

'Yes. I told him I wanted Rufus to be taught a lesson.'

'Please continue.'

'I told Rhein I was running out of money and that I had deposited a final payment of £10,000 in a safety deposit box at Swiss Bank, in central London. I had arranged for him to collect the money by speaking to the manager. I made up the name Mr Razz. He would tell the manager he was Mr Razz. There would be no need to produce any identification. He would be given a key to the safety deposit box 105. He would take the money and that would be the end of our business together.'

'That is a lot of money, just to observe and rough up a person, is it not?'

'Yes. I just wanted it done with.'

'No more questions, my lord.'

'Mr Pope, do you wish to question the witness?' asked Mr Justice Jacobs.

'Yes, my lord.'

Mr Pope QC was on his feet ready to unpick the defence team's evidence.

'Miss Rainford, I shall begin with your alleged affair with Sir Rufus Holroyd as the rest of your evidence, in relation to the charges made against you, begins with this alleged relationship, according to you. Where did you meet Sir Rufus Holroyd?'

'At a Conservative Party dinner dance held at the Grosvenor Hotel, three years ago.'

'Are you a member of the Conservative Party?'

'No. I was invited by my friend Emma Fairchild and her parents. Mr Fairchild is a Conservative member of parliament.'

'So, it was from a meeting at the dinner dance that you allege love blossomed?'

'Yes.'

'Does it not seem strange to you that after having an affair for three years no one knew of it?'

'We were careful.'

'But, as a couple, did you not have friends?'

'We had to keep our relationship low key.'

'Low key? Don't you mean non-existent?'

'We were in a relationship for three years.' She was close to tears.

'Then how do you explain the fact that Sir Rufus Holroyd denies any suggestion of an affair and says that he, in fact, had only met you on one occasion at the said dinner dance?'

'He is lying.'

'I put it to you, Miss Rainford, that there can only be one of two explanations. Either that the affair is pure fantasy, as it is too bizarre to take seriously, or that you are deliberately fabricating this story to protect the identity of your fellow terrorists. Or could it be a combination of both?'

'No. I'm telling the truth.'

'Truth? You do not know the meaning of the word.'

Bowles jumped to his feet. 'My lord, I object to this line of questioning.'

'Continue,' the judge instructed Pope.

'Miss Rainford. Do you intend to continue to insult the intelligence of the jury and this court?'

'It's the truth.'

'Miss Rainford, who is Mr S Smith?'

'I do not know a Mr Smith. It's a fabrication. Rufus rented the apartment.'

'Who are you protecting? Is Mr Smith a part of the terrorist organisation?'

'I don't know a Mr Smith and I am not part of a terrorist organisation.'

'Miss Rainford, you are charged with incitement to murder, not with having an affair, be it fact or fantasy. You are charged with incitement to murder any number of members of the European Parliament, coming and going from central office in Brussels. Do you not realise the severity of the charge against you?'

He paused.

'You have now given the name of the woman who you say arranged a contact or, as it has been referred to throughout the trial, a hardman. I look forward to questioning this witness.

'Returning to Rhein, whom you say you met on Westminster Bridge, in order to give him a payment for services as yet not carried out. You said he took the package of cash from under your arm while you were looking out across the Thames?'

'Yes.'

'Instinctively, you turned to face Rhein, as he took the money from under your arm? What happened the moment you turned around?'

'We just looked at each other, then he walked away.'

'Didn't you worry you might never see him again?'

'It crossed my mind, but I trusted the person who had put me in touch with him.'

'Oh yes, until recently, the elusive friend. When he rang you the second time, in your statement you say "he was ringing from Brussels". How did you know he was in Brussels?'

'He said he was.'

'I see. When he rang you again, you told him that you wanted Sir Rufus roughed up, and that £10,000 in cash would be deposited by yourself, at the Swiss Bank, central London. That he should ask for the manager, who would give him a key to safety deposit box 105?'

'Yes.'

'You told Rhein to present to the manager as a Mr Razz. Was that a code name? Why not use the name you have been using throughout this trial, Rhein? After all, you stated that it wasn't his real name. It was a name he had given you. Am I right?'

'Yes.'

'Why do you think he gave you a name?'

'I don't know. He just said, you will know me as Rhein.'

'So now he has two names?'

'I just made the name up. Mr Razz.'

'Miss Rainford, another matter that I find confusing is how was Rhein supposed to get from Brussels to London to collect the money and then be back in Brussels to "rough up" Sir Rufus in such a short space of time?'

'That wasn't my problem. I had kept my end of the bargain.'

'I have no further questions, my lord.' Pope sat down.

Mr Bowles QC stood to announce his next witness.

'My lord, I call my next witness, Mr Charles, manager of Swiss Bank.'

Mr Charles entered the witness box.

'Mr Charles, do you recognise the woman in the dock?'

'Yes, sir. She came to the bank to ask if a Mr Razz had collected the contents from a safety deposit box at our bank.'

'What did you tell her?'

198

'I told her I had no knowledge of the arrangement made on behalf of a Mr Razz.'

'What happened next?'

'She told me she had made the arrangement with the manager, only days ago, and that she had signed an agreement for Mr Razz to be given the key to safety deposit box 105.'

'Did she?'

'I had never met this woman before and certainly hadn't done as she claims. I had, in fact, been at head office when she alleges speaking to a manager and using the safe deposit box.'

'On the day the arrangements were made, where were you, Mr Charles?'

'At a manager's meeting most of the day. I returned to my office late afternoon, 4 p.m. I hadn't been on the floor all day. I wasn't officially there, if you understand. I called in to ensure all was well at the bank. The following day, I was back at head office.'

'Is it possible another manager or person could have met with Miss Rainford?'

'No. None of my staff would have dealt with the alleged transaction without following the proper procedure. We would have paperwork, signed and countersigned.'

'Is it possible Miss Rainford was set up?'

'Certainly not by the staff at Swiss Bank.'

'No further questions, my lord.'

'Mr Pope?'

'Yes, my lord. Mr Charles, you are a reputable bank manager of twenty years. During this time, has such a situation ever occurred before?'

'Never.'

'You are quite certain that before the day Miss Rainford came to the bank to enquire about Mr Razz, and the safety deposit box, you had never met this woman before?'

'Absolutely certain.'

'One more question, Mr Charles. On that day, in your opinion, how did the defendant present?'

'Anxious, disorientated and troubled.'

'Thank you, Mr Charles. No more questions, my lord.'

Mr Justice Jacobs addressed the court.

'We will resume tomorrow morning at ten thirty.'

All stand. Judge Jacobs left the courtroom.

The press buzzed with excitement.

CHAPTER TWENTY-SEVEN

The defence team worked throughout the night. The solicitor and his team hired their own inquiry agent, Mr Stevens, in trying to find Rosalind Bartholomew. Magda had remembered Ros saying she lived in a small village in Berkshire. Council records for each village would have to be checked. If she did live in the Berkshire area, her name would be recorded on a council list.

The team scanned through all the council records. Stevens shouted, 'Bingo. Mr Lacy, we have found her.'

'Well done, Stevens, I knew I could depend on you.'

Excitedly, Mr Lacy rang Mr Bowles.

'Mr Bowles, sorry to ring in the middle of the night, but we have found Rosalind Bartholomew.'

'That's wonderful news.'

'I will travel down to Berkshire shortly, to pay the lady a visit. With any luck she will be a witness for the defence and in the witness box tomorrow. Carry on with the next witness at court. I will update you as soon as I can.'

'Great work, Mr Lacy.'

The following morning, Mr Bowles QC and Miss Frost met with Magda.

'I have some good news: the defence team have located Rosalind Bartholomew. She does live in Berkshire. Mr Lacy is on his way to see her this morning. Fingers crossed he can persuade her to testify on your behalf.'

'I hope she isn't angry with me.'

'Miss Rainford, you had no choice but to tell us about her. She could be the person to set the record straight.'

'Yes, I suppose you're right.'

'Our first witness this morning is Mrs Proctor, the receptionist at Lakeside Spa. She will confirm that you did contact them in order to find Rosalind Bartholomew. Are you ready to face the day, Magda?'

'Yes.'

'We will see you in court shortly.'

Bowles had no other choice than to treat Magda's account as being true and valid.

'My lord, I call Mrs Proctor.'

Mrs Proctor took the oath.

'Thank you for attending today, Mrs Proctor … Mrs Proctor, do you recognise the defendant?'

'Yes.'

'Where have you seen her before?'

'At Lakeside Spa, where I work as a receptionist.'

'Do you recall Miss Rainford contacting Lakeside Spa and requesting a message be passed on to a woman named Rosalind Bartholomew?'

'Yes.'

'Please tell the court your account of that call and conversation.'

'I was on duty at reception. Miss Rainford rang and asked for the telephone number and address of Mrs Bartholomew. I told her it was against our policy and regulations to pass on personal information of our members. I suggested I could pass on a message to Mrs Bartholomew. I told her I could jot down the message, but could not guarantee the lady would receive it.'

'Do you know if Mrs Bartholomew received the message?'

'I don't. Mrs Bartholomew didn't always attend the spa on the days that I was on duty. When the solicitor, Mr Lacy, contacted me, I made enquiries amongst my colleagues regarding the message, but they knew nothing about it. It might have been accidently thrown away. We are not responsible for passing on messages between clients.'

'Thank you, Mrs Proctor. No further questions, my lord.'

Mr Pope QC got to his feet. 'Mrs Proctor, did you at any time see the defendant and Mrs Bartholomew together?'

'It's hard to say. I'm not sure.'

'Just answer the question please.'

'No.'

'Thank you, Mrs Proctor. No further questions, my lord.'

'My lord, I call Rhiannon Roe,' said Mr Bowles QC.

Rhiannon Roe entered the witness box.

'Miss Roe, you are a journalist at the *London Standard*. Please tell the court how you became acquainted with the defendant.'

He could feel the case slipping away.

'She approached me while I was on a weekend break at the Lakeside health spa.'

'What did she say exactly?'

'I cannot remember word for word. Something along the lines of she had a major scoop for the newspaper I work for.'

'Please continue.'

'She described it as being a national scandal. She named Sir Rufus Holroyd as her lover of three years.'

'You wrote of these allegations in your column, did you not?'

'Yes.'

'So, you thought she was telling the truth?'

'Yes, I suppose I must have.'

'Did she present as someone who could have been mentally unbalanced?'

'No, not at the time.'

'Please answer yes or no.'

'No.'

'Please continue.'

'Our initial conversation was very brief. I later met with her formally in the lounge area. The interview lasted an hour. I didn't consider her mental state. But since that time, I have had time to think and recall her presenting as troubled.'

'May I remind you we are no longer discussing how the defendant presented at the time of your meeting nor what you have considered since. At the time she presented to you, a professional journalist, she appeared to be of sound mind?'

'I guess so.'

'You guess so? Miss Roe, you did print her story in your column.'

'Yes.'

'No further questions, my lord.'

Mr Pope QC rose from his seat.

'Miss Roe, am I right in thinking you have worked at the *London Standard* for three years and that your column is still in its infancy?'

'Yes, I was given the column six months ago.'

'You are a relatively young journalist, are you not?'

'I suppose so.'

'Therefore, I put it to the court that while being a good journalist, you do not have the experience that comes only with time served as a journalist, those who would have many years of life experience under their belt? Therefore, you would not have the experience to assess her mental state?'

'I don't know.'

'Do you agree that you acted hastily and some might say irresponsibly in printing the story in your column, without substantiating evidence?'

'Yes.'

'Am I right in thinking you are very lucky that you have still got a job?'

'Yes.'

'And my final question. Did the proprietor of the *London Standard* have an apology printed to Sir and Lady Holroyd, for the story in your column?'

'Yes.'

'No further questions, my lord.'

'Mr Bowles, sorry to ring you at home, again.'

'It's quite all right, Mr Lacy. How did it go with Mrs Bartholomew?'

'She has agreed to be a witness, but I am not sure about her.'

'Why?'

'I tried to engage with her but she was evasive. She said she didn't want to discuss anything until she was in the witness box, being questioned by you.'

'At least she agreed. See you tomorrow.'

The following morning, before going into the courtroom, Mr Bowles and Miss Frost went down to the cells to meet with Magda.

'Good news, Magda. Rosalind Bartholomew is in the witness box this morning.'

'Was she angry that I let her down?' Magda asked.

'No, not at all. Although, I have mixed feelings about her as a witness. Mr Lacy is concerned that she is giving very little away. But we have to take the risk, she is crucial to your evidence.'

The courtroom was full to its capacity.

'I call Mrs Rosalind Bartholomew.' There were audible gasps; everyone had been waiting for the mystery witness.

For a moment, Magda thought a mistake had been made. The woman who stood in the witness box looked nothing like Ros, not initially. Her height ... she looked shorter. Maybe she was wearing flat shoes. Where was the deep orange tan? This woman had a pale complexion. It was the same woman, only she looked younger, softer and demure. The brassy hair that had stuck out at the top of her head-wrap at the spa was gone. She had soft, short blonde hair and wore little make-up. It was not Ros.

Bowles moved towards the witness. 'Mrs Rosalind Bartholomew, you frequent Lakeside Spa, do you not?'

'Yes.' Her voice was gentle, almost a whisper.

Magda leaned forwards to get a better look, still confused by Ros's appearance.

'Do you recognise the defendant?'

Rosalind looked directly at Magda.

'No.'

Bowles's eyes widened. 'Again, Mrs Bartholomew, look closely. Do you recognise the defendant?'

'No. I am sorry but I don't.'

Chatter throughout the courtroom broke the silence.

Bowles flushed as he tried to maintain his composure. 'You are on oath, Mrs Bartholomew.'

'Yes, I have just sworn on the Bible to tell the truth. I have never seen this woman before.'

Bowles shot a look at Magda. 'No further questions, my lord.' He slumped into his chair.

It hadn't been just the defence team that had been working throughout the night, researching Mrs Bartholomew. The prosecution team had been investigating too.

Pope couldn't believe his good fortune. The defence team had got the witness here.

'Mrs Bartholomew, you have told the court that you do not know or recognise the defendant. I do not intend to continue with this line of questioning. However, I have one question I would like you to answer. Would you kindly tell the court to whom you are related?'

'Yes, of course. I am the sister of Lady Daphne Holroyd.'

'Therefore, you are the sister-in-law of Sir Rufus Holroyd?'

'Yes.'

'No more questions, my lord.'

'You may step down, Mrs Bartholomew.'

Mr Justice Jacobs addressed the court.

'We shall break for lunch and return for closing speeches at two o'clock, prompt.'

'All rise.'

Bowles was fuming as he sat with his junior and Magda in the court cell.

'I had no idea she was related to Rufus. Please believe me.'

'Magda, I am lost for words. I am sorry, but I am going to have to quickly work on my closing speech. Since our last witness, my speech to the jury will have to be adapted.'

They left the cell. Bowles would have to prepare a damage limitation closing speech.

Mr Pope QC stood before the jury and began his closing speech.

'Ladies and gentlemen of the jury, the final witness for the defence was none other than Rosalind Bartholomew, sister of Lady Daphne Holroyd, and sister-in-law of Sir Rufus Holroyd. Mrs Bartholomew swore on oath that she had never before seen the defendant. Is this not proof that the defendant's evidence is all lies?

'Would Mrs Bartholomew befriend a woman who was having an affair with her brother-in-law? Would she conspire with the defendant to have him followed and wounded?

'Would she be the kind of woman who associated with hardmen? Would such a woman as Mrs Bartholomew be in the business of arranging contacts with hardmen?

'No. Surely it is evident to you, as it is to me, that the defendant's account and evidence is ridiculous and untrue. By blighting the good name of the Holroyd family, she is attempting to conceal the terrorist organisation with which she, Magda Rainford, is involved. British justice cannot and will not be fooled, and all of you here today, ladies and gentlemen of the jury, are presently representative of British justice.

'Are you to be fooled by a terrorist? Are you going to allow this woman to insult your intelligence with deceit and untruths? Her entire evidence is a concoction of lies that has caused much pain to Sir Rufus Holroyd and his wife, and also caused anguish to Mrs Bartholomew.'

Pope glanced around the courtroom.

'There can surely only be one verdict. Guilty. It is your civil duty as upright citizens to ensure justice prevails today. It is your duty to your fellowman and to keeping the streets of Britain and Europe safe from terrorist activity to find the defendant, Magda Rainford, guilty. Thank you.'

He returned to his seat. The courtroom was silent.

Mr Bowles QC addressed the jury.

'Magda Rainford believes every word she has told us. Whether or not it is accurate, we cannot know for sure. The defendant is without family or friends and whether she did have an affair with Sir Rufus, or whether it was a fantasy, it was very real to her.

'Is Miss Rainford a terrorist? Or is she a lonely individual caught up in something outside her control?

'Today, you the jury must decide whether or not Magda Rainford is guilty of the charge of incitement to murder.

'Thank you.'

Mr Justice Jacobs addressed the jury.

'Ladies and gentlemen, this has been an unusual trial and a disturbing one. It is for you to analyse and question the evidence that has been presented to you throughout the trial. If you have any concerns or questions that will assist you in your deliberations, I will be pleased to answer them for you. It is your responsibility to decide whether or not the defendant, Magda Rainford, is guilty of the charge of incitement to murder. You may now retire to consider your verdict.'

'All rise.'

In her cell at Holloway prison, awaiting the verdict, Magda reflected on the day. Until the silence was broken.

'Hey, Magda, you're on TV. Well, the van you were in is. It'll be on again later; you can see it then,' said Cindy.

'I don't want to see or hear the news. I have been in court every day listening to it.'

Cindy was pacing around, whilst Magda lay on her bunk and wished Cindy would shut up.

'Joan, my sister, has got a visiting order. She knows I'm sharing a cell with you – she'll want the low-down on what you're like, the nosey cow.'

Magda said nothing.

'How did it go at the end, I mean, did you have a tough-looking jury?'

'It didn't go well. The jury didn't like me.'

'Are you a terrorist, Mags?'

'No, sorry to disappoint, but for the hundredth time, I am not a terrorist.'

'Still, if you're found guilty, then that would make you one.'

'If you say so.'

'This Rufus fella, was he really everything you said he was?'

'I thought so.'

'You could write a book. Eh, I could write a book about my time inside, sharing a cell with a terrorist. Or a newspaper deal, what do you think?'

'Do what you like.'

'I wonder where they will send you once you're convicted. Miles away probably.'

'I could be found not guilty.'

'I doubt it, love. Even I think you're guilty, but we're still mates?'

CHAPTER TWENTY-EIGHT

Magda was taken to court every day awaiting the verdict. She sat in the court cell waiting to hear her fate.

Friday afternoon.

'The jury are back with a verdict.' The prison officer led Magda from the cell up to the courtroom and into the dock.

'All rise.'

Mr Justice Jacobs entered the courtroom.

'Be seated.'

The court clerk asked, 'Ladies and gentlemen of the jury, have you made a decision?'

'Yes, my lord.'

'Would the defendant stand.'

Magda stood and looked at the jury.

'Would the foreman of the jury please stand.'

'Do you find the defendant, Miss Magda Rainford, guilty or not guilty on incitement to murder?'

'Guilty, my lord.'

Magda felt faint and broke into a cold sweat. She reached for the wooden stand in front of her, to maintain her balance.

The journalists rushed towards the exit.

Mr Justice Jacobs spoke. 'I would like to thank the ladies and gentlemen of the jury. I shall adjourn sentencing. Take the defendant down.'

'All rise.'

Mr Justice Jacobs left the courtroom.

Magda was led back downstairs.

In the robing room Pope joined Bowles as they changed their clothing.

'Good work, Bowles, you did your best with little evidence.'

'Congratulations, Pope, another win for you.'

Bowles just wanted to get away from court. He had arranged to meet Miss Frost at a wine bar. A few barristers from their chambers were joining them to commiserate.

After a couple of glasses of wine, Bowles reflected on the case. Magda didn't strike him as being a terrorist or having the nous to be involved in an organised plot. She had fretted because she betrayed a promise.

A lot of things didn't add up, but without the evidence and witnesses, well …

He had fulfilled his brief, the jury had found her guilty, it was out of his hands. The case was over.

Mr Justice Jacobs requested two psychiatric assessments, prior to passing sentence. He would hold a hearing where Dr Poulson would give his professional opinion before the court. He wanted to ensure he sentenced in the interest of the public and the defendant.

Returning to Holloway prior to sentencing, Magda knew she was finished.

'Hey, you're back, you just missed yourself on TV, again.'

'I keep telling you, Cindy, I have no wish to see it.'

'They found you guilty, girl. So, you're a terrorist.'

'I'm not.'

'The jury said guilty. Just think, I share a cell with the infamous Magda Rainford. Now, that book we was talking about—'

'Go ahead, write it.'

'How much do you think I'd get?'

'Oh, Cindy, go away.'

'My mates on the outside want the goss on you.'

'I'm having a rest, so either be quiet or leave me in peace.'

Magda got back into the prison routine. This was it. But how long for?

After breakfast, a prison officer approached Magda.

'Magda, the psychiatrist is here wanting to see you. Let's go.'

Everyone was watching as Magda was led off the wing, and taken into the office block. She was sick of these people prying into her life.

'Miss Rainford, I am Dr Poulson, please sit down.'

Magda sat across from Dr Poulson, a large table between them.

'You understand why we are meeting?'

She nodded.

'I am here to assess you on behalf of the court, which will help the judge determine your sentence. Shall we begin?'

Dr Poulson asked Magda to give an account of her early years and the death of her parents. He recognised the lasting impact this had had on her.

'The death of your parents has left gaps in your emotional development and has enhanced your feelings of abandonment throughout your life.'

He, like the rest of society, thought that the story of her relationship with Rufus Holroyd was pure fantasy.

'Due to your abandonment issues in childhood, you have craved attention from a parental figure all your life. Am I right?'

'I missed having parents.'

'Consider this, let's suppose we take your story of a relationship with Sir Rufus Holroyd as true.'

'It is true.'

'Please, bear with me. As you were growing up, did you have an image of the type of man you would fall in love with?'

'Yes.'

'An older, established man. A father figure, for example.'

'I always wanted to meet someone special, who would love and care for me.'

'Someone like Sir Rufus?'

'Yes.'

'I think this relationship you conjured up is a way of making the past wrongs right. A means of reclaiming the love from the father figure by proxy. Sir Rufus Holroyd meets the criteria of the fantasy figure of Magda the child. The criteria would have been modified over the years, to meet the current needs of Magda the young woman.'

'I fell in love with the man.'

'I have no doubt you believe you did. Sir Rufus denies your story and describes you as a fantasist.'

'He is lying. Everything happened the way I said it did.'

'Sir Rufus, being a public figure and an older man, was an ideal choice. It could have easily been someone else with similar attributes.'

'No. I had a three-year relationship with Rufus.'

Dr Poulson paused and tapped his pen. 'If you love him so much, why would you have him roughed up, physically hurt?'

'I wanted him to realise I wasn't going away. I wanted him to take notice of me.'

'What if everybody who had a relationship breakdown chose to take the line you did?'

'Ours is a special love. Other people got in the way.'

'Who?'

'His wife.'

'She was there before you. Perhaps it was you who was in the way.'

'You simply don't understand what we had.'

Dr Poulson thought Miss Rainford lacked the ability to reason. She couldn't see the situation from another perspective. This lack of judgement posed a risk to anyone who didn't comply with her chosen outcome. Worst of all, she could not distinguish between fact and fantasy.

Dr Poulson pulled out a piece of paper from his file.

'I received this from your GP.'

He read aloud the medication she had been prescribed. 'Sleeping tablets 10mg. Diazepam 5mg. Anti-depressants – Prozac.'

'I was a nervous wreck. I couldn't sleep, I had no one to turn to. He visited less often. I thought I was losing him. I was desperate.'

He asked a few more questions and studied her non-verbal communication. He watched her facial expressions and body language.

With a diagnosis ready for the court hearing with Justice Jacobs, he brought the session to a close.

'Miss Rainford, we have come to the end of the assessment. Therefore, there will be no need for a further meeting.' He went to the door and knocked on the glass panel.

'We are finished here.'

The prison officer escorted Magda from the room. Dr Poulson did not acknowledge either of them as they left.

Magda knew she was at the mercy of these professionals and that she was under the microscope, not as a person but an object of analysis. She was the loneliest person in the world.

She lay on her lower bunk and closed her eyes. The interview had exhausted her. Day after day and week after week there had been constant discussions of her childhood and relationships. Tired of it all, she wanted to sleep.

'Mags, come on. It's dinner time.'

'Cindy, do you have to be so loud?'

'You're always in some meditative state, whenever I come into this cell. You need to wake up, girl. Come on.'

'I'm not hungry.'

'I won't let you starve yourself. You are going to have a long stretch in front of you, years, decades, so come on, let's go. I won't let you do anything daft while on my watch.'

'Like what?'

'Starve yourself to death.'

'I'll just get stared at. I want to be left alone.'

'They look at you because you are big in here, Mrs Big. Compared to these losers, you are queen of the castle.' Cindy put her cigarette out. 'I wish I had your rep. I'd milk it for all it's worth.' She paused. 'But I wouldn't want the sentence you'll get. Come on.'

'Okay, but I am not answering any more, bloody questions about terrorism.'

Magda fluctuated between feeling grounded and being in a state of confusion. Her mood was controlled by medication; that had been increased. She still struggled to believe she was really in prison, but when Cindy started mouthing off, she knew she was inside.

A couple of days later, Magda was escorted off the wing again to meet with the second psychiatrist.

'Hello, Miss Rainford, I am a psychiatrist, Dr James Stone. I suppose you knew I would be visiting you.'

'Yes, I've already seen one psychiatrist.'

'I have read your file and know your childhood history. May I suggest we start with you telling me about the situation you find yourself in at the present time?'

'The reason I find myself where I am is because of my love for Rufus. What started as a love affair has become a nightmare.'

'Please continue. Let's focus on what led you to where you are today.'

'You know it all, just read the court transcript.'

'I want your version of events. This is about you, not the trial.'

'I met Rufus for the first time at the dinner dance and was immediately attracted to him. I was introduced to him and later in the evening we had a conversation.'

'What kind of conversation?'

'Quite flirty, a lot of eye contact, I saw him watching me throughout the evening. After that meeting I thought about him all the time.'

'What happened next?'

'I received a letter on Houses of Parliament stationery, inviting me to join him there, for a guided tour of the place. I thought it was just a kindly gesture. Why would he be interested in me? I was a little disappointed … I was very disappointed, to be honest.'

'That it wasn't a date?'

She nodded.

'Please, carry on.'

'I went. He gave me a tour of the building. We had coffee in his official office. I thanked him and was about to leave when he suggested an early dinner. It was all very casual. We had a lovely evening, after which we exchanged telephone numbers and went on our way.'

'How did you feel?'

'Optimistic. He clearly liked me and wanted to meet again.'

'Moving forward, you moved to Chelsea and became his, for want of a better expression, kept woman?'

'I suppose I was. I always thought we would be together as a couple. We both invested heavily in our relationship.'

'But you invested the most from what I have read.'

'I gave up everything – work, friends, my home.'

'But you remained there.'

'I wasn't going to give up on us. Even when he wanted to end it, he pretended it was for my benefit, so I could start a new life. I didn't buy it.'

'Have you ever considered that it was for your benefit?'

'No. Rufus was my life blood. I wasn't going to let him go.'

'I understand your commitment, but if one party wishes to end a relationship, surely they should be allowed to.'

'It was because of his guilt, his wife, the lies he had to tell.'

'What if he was telling you the truth and he had had enough?'

'You cannot understand how it was. The Rufus I knew would never give up on us.'

Dr Stone listened. He gave her space to share her feelings.

'I'm sorry for being tearful. It's not about my incarceration, it's only for my love of Rufus. I feel such loneliness, isolation, and despair at being abandoned by him.'

'What if I told you that I would link your intense sorrow and abandonment issues raised by the Rufus scenario with the perceived abandonment of you by your parents?'

'I wouldn't feel this way about anyone but him. This is about him, not the past.'

'Have you ever heard of transference?'

'No.'

'In your case, transferring the internalised loss of love from your parents to your love for Sir Rufus, and his love for you. All the revenge you supressed, wanting to hurt your parents for abandoning you in the past. These negative thoughts and feelings you had for your parents transferred to Sir Rufus. So, when things were not going the way you wanted, it was "look out, Rufus."

'As a child you were powerless, you suppressed your anger towards them in order to survive. Now as an adult you have power and you exercised that power against Sir Rufus. The situation, however, became exaggerated and more life-threatening to you because of the buried anger and fear.

'The abandonment and his withdrawal of love and support enabled these buried feelings to re-emerge. Remember, Magda, the strong unexpressed feelings we push down inside us don't just go away, they fester and wait for an opportunity, a time when they can be given expression.'

Magda found much of what he said made sense to her.

'Yes, it feels right, here.' She pressed the palm of her hand against her solar plexus. 'I did hate my parents for leaving me, but I never hated Rufus, not real hate.'

'That is because Sir Rufus isn't dead, he is still here, so there was still a chance of getting him back and getting your needs met. Have you heard the quote, "When I was a child, I thought like a child"?'

'Yes.'

'Whenever you thought Rufus was abandoning you, you thought like a child. You boomeranged back into the past.'

Initially, Dr Stone had thought her story of a romantic relationship with Rufus was fantasy, but he noted a consistency in her story. She had a knowledge and insight into her subject that a fantasist would lack. Not once had she become florid or irrational. Some of the things she described did sound elaborate, exaggerated, even grandiose, but the sessions demonstrated this was part of her childlike perception and adulation of this father figure, Rufus – the idealised father figure. Could it be that she couldn't bear to have the innocent love she had to give once again cast aside in such a brutal way?

Dr Stone concluded that Rufus had promised to be all the things her father had been unable to be: protective, paternal, loving and caring. Rufus was also powerful, enigmatic and intelligent, someone who she believed would give her the security she had never had.

Whether or not the relationship with Rufus was real or fantasy, it was clear to Dr Stone that her parents' deaths were linked to her actions that followed the perceived abandonment by Rufus. He was the object of her love, her champion, her saviour. He concluded it was a case of transference, of stored childhood feelings onto Rufus, in the present time.

Dr Stone struggled to accept Magda's insistence that she hired a contact, this hardman, via a woman she barely knew or as it turns out didn't know at all.

Magda's explanation of the hired contact or hardman seemed messy and unprofessional, both on her side and on the side of the man she referred to as Rhein. The man shot dead by police who was part of a terrorist organisation.

'How did you come to hire the contact?'

'You know already. Ros, Mrs Bartholomew, arranged it.'

'You are sticking to this story, even though she clearly stated she never had any association with you.'

'It is the truth. She arranged for him to contact me by telephone and the rest, as they say, is history.'

'Why go down this road?'

'Desperation. She, Ros, encouraged me to take back power. I thought she was my friend.'

'You told the police you had spoken to this terrorist a number of times on the telephone and met him on Westminster Bridge. Why did you say this?'

'It's the truth.'

Again, he noted that this was very real to her. The jury had found her guilty of incitement to murder. He believed Magda Rainford could not differentiate between fact and fantasy. What troubled him was that he thought the fantasy and the fiction were the wrong way round. Her explanation of the relationship with Sir Rufus had consistency and reference to specific experiences between them, the factual story. The fantasy was the involvement in a terrorist plot. Magda had put herself in the frame by admitting to knowing and having an agreement with Rhein, the terrorist.

Dr Stone didn't feel prison was the right place for Magda. She needed ongoing assessments. She needed to be taken care of.

Returning to court for sentencing, Magda knew she wouldn't be going back to Holloway prison. She had said her farewells to Cindy and prison staff.

Prior to sentence being passed, Mr Justice Jacobs heard evidence from Dr Poulson. He discussed the intricacies of the assessment to ensure that the correct judgement was made on where she would carry out her sentence and the restrictions upon her release in due course.

Dr Poulson had a long and distinguished career in psychiatry and had worked on behalf of the court for decades. The assessment by Dr Stone was also taken into consideration.

Mr Justice Jacobs rose for a short time to consider the sentence, having heard the submissions of counsel.

'All rise.'

Mr Justice Jacobs entered the courtroom.

'Will the defendant please stand?'

'Magda Rainford, having considered the psychiatric evidence from Dr Poulson and Dr Stone, I have concluded, because of your mental health, that prison is not an option at the present time. Due to the diagnosis and issues raised in the reports, I have decided that you should be taken to Ashworth high security hospital in Merseyside. You will be detained there for an indefinite period. There will be a restriction order under the Mental Health Act, which means that you will not be released into the community until it is concluded by a panel that it is safe to do so.

'It is my hope that you will receive the support and care you need. The defendant may leave the court.'

'All rise.'

It was over.

CHAPTER TWENTY-NINE

Rufus and Daphne had been back in England for a week and continued to be besieged by the press. Rufus's mood had changed radically and he ignored the journalists.

'Rufus, darling, I wish you would talk to me.'

'I don't want to keep discussing the same thing over and over. You must understand that?'

She reached out to hold him but he shrugged her away.

'Please, Daphne, I am busy.'

She approached him again and touched his arm; she could feel his body tense.

'Why don't you go for a walk with the dogs?'

'Won't you tell me what is troubling you so much?'

'You have to ask?'

'What did the Prime Minister have to say when you saw him last?'

'Let me make myself clear. I do not wish to discuss, share or talk about anything.'

'Why not just tell me what he said?'

'Right. He said he hoped that I wasn't another Conservative politician who was going to make a mockery of his "back to basics" policy. Now are you happy?'

'But it wasn't true. Didn't you tell him that it wasn't true?'

'I have told the world it wasn't true. I can't help it if the Prime Minister doesn't believe me.'

'Why won't he believe you?'

'Ask him yourself. Now, would you please leave me in peace?'

'You spend more time with Cedric Bowes-Water than me.'

'Oh, please stop this nonsense.'

'You confide in Cedric. He knows more than I do. Do you know how ridiculous that makes me feel? You have Cedric, I have no one.'

'I'm going to my study.' He slammed the door behind him.

Why was he behaving like this?

Daphne had been perturbed to hear her sister, Rosalind, had been called as a witness for the defence. Even more perplexing was that the papers reported Rosalind had no evidence to give other than she didn't know this woman Magda Rainford.

Daphne's imagination was running wild. What if Rufus had had an affair with the woman and Rosalind knew all along? No, that was nonsense. The press had reported Rosalind didn't know Magda Rainford. But how did Magda Rainford know she had a sister? Why would a terrorist suspect call Rosalind to be a witness for the defence? Perhaps this Magda was obsessed with Rufus? Or maybe she had researched the family and they were being used as a cover for her terrorist activities? This seemed to be a logical answer. Was Rufus troubled because he believed them both to be in danger? Perhaps Rufus had been the terrorist target not MEPs in general.

'It's driving me crazy,' she cried.

CHAPTER THIRTY

Magda was taken immediately from court to Merseyside in the North of England, to start her sentence at Ashworth high security hospital.

Once she had been through the admission procedure she was escorted to a women's unit. She was pleased to find everyone had a room to themselves. The row of rooms was overseen by the nursing station.

'Welcome to unit one, Magda. All patients' room doors are kept open, until lock-up in the evening. The bed, table and chair are securely fastened to the floor and no items are allowed that could be used as a weapon.'

'The room is basic but not as bleak as a prison cell,' Magda answered.

'This is your home now. We want you to be as comfortable as possible. The psychiatric nurses' station overlooks the entire patient area. The walls of the entire office consist of smash-proof glass. Come this way.'

They walked to the left of the bedrooms.

'The TV room is functional but it has to be. The TV is mounted high on the wall so no one can reach it, and there is a payphone in the corner. Again, furniture, chairs and tables cannot be moved. These too are securely attached to the floor. The TV room also has a wall of safety glass – this allows us to see and monitor patients. It is a bit of a fish bowl but you will get used to it. It is for everyone's safety.'

'So, we are visible twenty-four hours a day?'

'Not during the night when you are in your room. This is no ordinary hospital, safety and security are our priority.'

The nursing staff were friendly but diligent at all times. They never let their guard down.

'Do not turn your back on a fellow patient. This is advised in case of attack. Keep everyone in view. There have been cases where even elderly patients have attempted to strangle a fellow patient from behind.'

Magda found it depressing that some of the patients had been in the hospital for twenty and thirty years. Their crimes were not discussed, but sometimes it was obvious who they were, from TV and newspaper reports in the past. They were killers.

Why had she been put in a place with serial killers, with women who were clearly very disturbed? Long days of being cooped up together did cause a lot of unpredictable and bizarre behaviour. The long-termers were institution-alised, round and round they would walk, never speaking. They just stared ahead. At any time, someone could lunge out and do serious physical damage. Medication was the key – sedatives and anti-psychotic drugs kept most patients mellow.

'We have a small, secure outdoor area where patients can have a smoke or take the fresh air. Ignore the helicopter that hovers overhead sometimes. They are hoping to get a photograph of one of our more notorious patients.'

Surprisingly, Magda was sleeping well and felt safe and comfortable in her room.

'Do I call you Nurse Claire or Claire?'

'Claire will do.'

'Is it possible to see a doctor? I don't feel right.'

'Our resident psychiatrist is visiting the unit on Wednesday. You are already on his list.'

'These anti-psychotic drugs make me feel out of touch with reality.'

'I can't change the medication. Dr Walker will assess you on Wednesday and will decide if the dosage needs changing. Aren't they keeping you calm?'

'I feel numb.'

'You would feel far worse without them. It is a shock to the system being placed at this hospital. The medication will ease you into your new life here with us.'

The radio was broadcast throughout the ward at various times of the day, one being rest period, when all the patients returned to their rooms at 2.30 p.m. Usually, it was classical music, which helped to keep everyone calm. Magda loved the classical music station, the memories of her time with Rufus would drift into her mind. It was another lifetime. The memories remained but not the feelings associated with them. She felt no emotion.

CHAPTER THIRTY-ONE

Four months on, during the afternoon rest period, a nurse came to Magda's doorway.

'Magda, you have a visitor. Come with me.'

Magda dragged her heavily sedated body from the bed and shuffled her way along the corridor. Doors had to be unlocked and then locked behind them all through the building until they were out of the unit and into an office. Inside stood a man about forty-five years of age, formally dressed.

'I will wait outside.' Magda was surprised that the nurse had left her alone with the man.

'Miss Rainford, are you okay?'

'Yes, I was asleep, just coming round.'

'I shall come straight to the point of my visit. I am here on behalf of Sir Rufus Holroyd.'

'Rufus?'

'I am just the messenger, you understand. I have been instructed to tell you that Sir Rufus is engaged in talks to ensure your release from Ashworth. If or when you are released, you will be given a new identity and be relocated somewhere in Britain where no one knows you. Under no circumstances must you ever make contact with Sir Rufus again.'

'But—'

'Or you will find yourself back here. On no account must you discuss my visit with anyone.'

'But—'

'I have nothing further to say. I am simply the messenger. Good day to you.'

The man left the room and the nurse returned to escort Magda back to the unit. No questions were asked, nothing was said.

Eventually, Magda questioned if the visit had actually happened; fortunately, staff assured her the visit had taken place.

Rufus still cared for her and he wouldn't let her down. He wouldn't let her rot in this hell hole. She had hope for a future now, a future without him. She knew she would have to abide by what the man had said.

Time to let Rufus go. If he cared enough to assist in her release then she must set him free.

It was Dr Walker's second ward round. He greeted Magda with a smile.

'I must say, Magda, I am encouraged by the feedback from the staff team. You are doing very well. Are you finding the change to your medication effective?'

'Yes. I don't feel detached anymore.'

'Nurse Kennedy informs me you are reading, listening to music and have taken an interest in your hygiene and appearance.'

'I want to be as normal as I can be.'

'What are you reading?'

'I have a book on psychotherapy, I hope to understand myself better.'

'I am sure we can get you more self-help books. What else do you like to read?'

'Historical fiction.'

'When you read, do you find you are able to absorb the information and recall the story when you return to it?'

'Yes. The hours fly by.'

Dr Walker paused. 'You realise you won't be leaving here any time soon?'

'Oh, yes. Just trying to make the most of each day.'

'I am very impressed with your progress. Keep up the good work.'

'Thank you.'

Magda smiled to herself as she left the room. *Oh, but I will be leaving here, Dr Walker.*

At the end of the ward round Dr Walker met with the nursing team.

'Magda Rainford must remain on close observation. At some point it will hit her that she is here possibly for life. We don't want any suicides on the unit.'

Magda joined the art group. Three times a week, patients were escorted to the craft room, where they could paint, draw, have pottery lessons. These art sessions were facilitated by two art therapists. Magda loved these classes.

'Magda, you have shown so much promise in your art work. I find this painting interesting – can you tell me what it is telling us?'

'I think so.'

'This man and woman, is the woman you?'

'Yes.'

'You have almost painted the woman but not fully?'

'Because she hasn't become whole yet. She still has to grow as a human being.'

'And the man, he is mostly an outline, why?'

'I won't be painting him as he is fading into the distance.'

'Is he leaving? Or are you leaving him?'

'I'm letting him go.'

'That is a brave thing to do.'

'It's the right thing to do?'

'The only thing to do.'

Patients on the unit were challenging, most were psychopaths and sociopaths and spent their time aimlessly walking around. They would try to freak out a member of staff by their behaviour; they would challenge staff with deliberate unsettling conversation – goading, jabbering relentlessly into the face of a nurse in an attempt to instil fear and cause the nurse to become overwhelmed, lose control and panic. If this happened, other patients took advantage of the situation and would join in and surround the nurse, in an attempt to make them crack. Patients were manipulative and dangerous; any weakness or uncertainty would be picked up on immediately. Some took great pleasure in scaring staff. It was all a game. They lacked consciences and would go to any length to entertain themselves at the expense of the people who were there to help them. Staff always had each other's backs – a newer member of staff would be singled out, and so would be shadowed by an experienced colleague. Magda kept to her room unless she was due to attend art class or see the psychiatrist. She would walk to the outdoor area, but mainly she stayed away from everyone. The only thing that kept her going was the knowledge that she wasn't in there forever.

It was a Wednesday afternoon rest period. Magda lay on her bed and relaxed as she listened to the classical music she had come to enjoy so much; it made her feel closer to Rufus, and closer to freedom. There was a sudden interruption of the programme.

'We interrupt *Classical Music Daily* for an important news bulletin.

'Shock waves have passed through the political world today on the reporting of the assassination of the prominent MEP Sir Rufus Holroyd and his wife, Daphne. They were shot dead while leaving a function in central Brussels late last night. The gunman got away and there is no further news at present. The gunman opened fire as the couple approached their car. The police will release a statement later today. Sir Rufus was a highly respected man who will be remembered for his political zeal as well as his work and support for numerous charities ...'

Magda lay still and tried to process the information she had just heard. *Is this real?* Has this actually happened? It couldn't have.

The newspapers covered the story of the assassination and speculated that the already incarcerated Miss Rainford was linked to the murderous organisation. The report said, *'Miss Rainford had refused to cooperate with the police and this had probably signed Sir Rufus's death warrant.'*

The Prime Minister, John Major, read out a statement in the Commons. 'The terrorist organisation who have committed this abomination will be hunted down and brought to justice.'

A news frenzy continued for months and the name 'Magda Rainford' became synonymous with terrorism. The newspapers were all saying the same thing.

'There would be a public outcry and damnation should Magda Rainford ever be considered for release by the prison review panel.'

Sir Rufus and Daphne Holroyd had a joint funeral. A quiet affair, at Barnston Green parish church.

A number of distinguished mourners attended the funeral and the press wanted photographs to fill the Sunday papers. The press maintained a respectful distance.

The eulogy was read by Cedric Bowes-Water, who paid tribute to his good friend Rufus. He finished by saying, 'It is somewhat comforting that Rufus and Daphne have passed over together, albeit under such dreadful circumstances. They were, after all, a devoted couple.

'We give thanks that we knew them, our lives enriched by their friendship.

'Farewell, dear friends.'

* * *

A year on and no organisation had come forwards to take responsibility for the murders of Sir Rufus and Daphne Holroyd. The police in Britain and Brussels ran out of leads on the case. To quell the predicted public outcry and the lack of confidence in the government's ability to ensure public safety, there had to be an inquiry. The eventual release of the inquiry some eight months later didn't bring to the fore anything that wasn't already known. Someone had to be seen to pay for the crime. No further investigation was to be carried out in finding the gunman who murdered the Holroyds. The Prime Minister wanted it finished. The entire case had been a political embarrassment and therefore Magda Rainford would remain at Ashworth Hospital for an indefinite period.

Magda retreated into a silent world, unable or unwilling to communicate with anyone. The psychiatric team continued to monitor her and she was placed on a high dosage of medication as it was feared she might attempt to take her own life.

Life went on in the outside world, new stories, new headlines. The assassination was yesterday's news.

* * *

It had taken two years to execute the last will and testimony of Sir Rufus and Daphne Holroyd. It was an old will, that they had made when they were much younger and hopeful for the future and their family.

CHAPTER THIRTY-TWO

The engines spun into life as the private jet made its way towards the runway. Strapped securely in her seat, the elegant, solitary woman looked out the window as the plane began to move along the runway faster and faster until it lifted off the ground. Higher and higher it climbed.

Rosalind Bartholomew continued to take in the view of England's green and pleasant land until it disappeared below the clouds.

'Farewell to all that.' She smiled.

Rosalind was now a multi-millionaire. She had inherited everything Sir Rufus and Daphne had possessed. There had been no children, and as she was Daphne's only sister, she was the next of kin.

Rosalind had sold off the entire estate and its total value had been deposited into her Swiss account. She was on her way to start a new life in a more exotic climate.

No, she would not be returning to England. She had what she wanted, what she had waited for.

As she settled back in her seat, Rosalind was poured a glass of champagne by the stewardess. It mirrored how she was feeling: sparkling and full of life.

Lindy, as she always preferred to be called, raised her glass and made a silent toast.

To Daphne, my ever-so-perfect sister who always got what she wanted, well dear, you got what you deserved. To Rufus, the man who betrayed my love so many years ago, you chose to be with Daphne, and so it is only right you die alongside her.

Last but not least, Miss Magda Rainford, without whom none of this would have been possible.

'I toast you all.

EPILOGUE

Three years into her sentence, Magda received a visitor.

'Miss Rainford. Do you remember me?'

Magda looked at the man. 'Should I?'

'I'm Dr Stone, the psychiatrist. I assessed you on behalf of the court.'

'Oh, yes, you helped put me in here.'

'I have thought a lot about you over the years. Especially when Rufus and Daphne Holroyd were murdered in Brussels.'

'Please don't ask if I will agree to collaborate on a book about my life.'

'Absolutely not. If you would just hear me out …?'

They both sat down.

'No terrorist organisation ever came forward to take responsibility for the murders.'

'Because there was no terrorist organisation.'

'I believe you.'

'You do?'

He nodded. 'The whole investigation seemed to be dead in the water. Something wasn't right about the lack of input and interest in resolving the case.'

Magda leaned towards Dr Stone. 'I did have a three-year relationship with Rufus.'

'I believe that too.'

Magda gave a deep sigh. 'But it changes nothing for me.'

'It could do. Did you know that Rosalind Bartholomew was sole beneficiary to the Holroyd's estate? On their death, the estate passed to her. They had no children – Rosalind was next of kin. She sold up and left the country, lock, stock and barrel.'

'Are you saying she played me?'

'She certainly did.'

'But why?'

'I traced an old university friend of Rufus's. He told me that Rufus was in a relationship with Rosalind, or Lindy, as she was referred to then. Rufus left her for her sister, Daphne. The friend, Robert Clark, told me Lindy and her sister became estranged and that Lindy always loved Rufus. He seems to think Lindy probably always intended to take revenge.'

Magda became angry.

'I thought she was my friend.'

'It was nothing personal. You were a pawn in the game. A crucial pawn.'

'This is all hearsay, it changes nothing.'

'At the moment, no. There has to be someone, a common link. Rosalind must have taken a keen interest in the Holroyds' marriage from a distance. She knew about you before you even met her.'

'I was so stupid.'

'You were young and naive. I want to get an investigator onto it.'

'You would do this for me?'

'For justice. I feel a burden of guilt for you being here. I was never comfortable with the charge made against you, I never thought you were a terrorist.'

The two of them sat in silence, absorbing the information. Dr Stone stood up, ready to go. 'Leave it with me.'

'Thank you for believing me, and thank you for what you are doing.'

Magda returned to the unit with a glimmer of hope. She was older and wiser. She trusted Dr Stone. He was a decent man and he believed her.

And she believed in him.

ABOUT THE AUTHOR

Julie Conrad lives in Cheshire with her husband and three Pomeranian dogs. With a long career as a social worker in London boroughs before returning to the north west to practice. In 1997 she became a Regulatory Inspector for an Inspection unit now CQC.

BA[Hons]Social Science degree plus CQSW. Middlesex University.

BA[Hons}Regulation and Inspection. University of Salford.

An acrylic artist, member of the Altrincham Society of Artists for ten years. Julie has had two private exhibitions as well as exhibiting with the ASA.

Loves all animals and wildlife, gardening, growing vegetables and very tall tulips.

An avid fitness fan for over forty years. Julie remains a vibrant, creative person who promotes and supports animal welfare, RSPCA, PETA, and kindness to all.